RUNNING HOT

Published in 2006 by Simply Read Books
www.simplyreadbooks.com

Text © 2005 David Hill
Cover photograph © Jack Newton

First published in 2005 by Mallinson Rendel Publishers Ltd.

Cataloguing in Publication Data

Hill, David, 1942-
        Running hot / David Hill.

ISBN 10: 1-894965-52-3
ISBN-13: 978-1-894965-52-1

        I. Title.

PZ7.H5379Ru 2006   j823'.914   C2006-900136-7

Cover design by Hamish Thompson
Interior page design by Scott Polzen
Printed in the USA

10 9 8 7 6 5 4 3 2 1

RUNNING HOT

DAVID HILL

SIMPLY READ BOOKS

ONE

The last, thumb-thick pine branch broke off and sailed down onto the others lying on the ground. Garth Muir lowered his pruning saw and pushed back his fiberglass hard hat. He rubbed his nose where pine pollen had gotten up it, pulled at the neck of his T-shirt where pine needles had gotten down it, picked at the arm of his wool sweater where pine resin had gotten smeared across it. "Two hundred and six!" he yelled.

Around him, the other saplings shook as more pruning saws sliced at them. "Two hundred and seven!" called Danny Marsich. Garth's friend stepped out into the open, kicking sawn-off branches out of the way. He grinned at Garth, pulled a granola bar from his jacket pocket and started chomping into it. Among the slender nine-foot trees on either side, arms kept sawing.

Garth took off his work gloves and shook pine needles out of them. He'd even found the prickly things in his boxers last night. He hadn't told anyone – of course – except Danny. Then Danny – of course – told everyone.

1

The two boys gazed back down the rows of freshly-pruned saplings. Slim gray trunks shone in the sun. It was like looking down an avenue that dipped and rose over the rough ground towards the forestry road from which they'd started.

"Two hundred and eight," said Hinu Katene's soft voice.

"Two hundred and nine!" bawled Kelsey Brooking's unsoft voice.

Garth looked up as something moved above. A chickadee flicked past, side-slipping and darting after the insects shaken from the pine saplings. "Should charge him for lunch," Danny said.

Garth grinned. Trust Danny to be thinking about lunch, even after he'd had it. Higher up, a crow flashed towards tall, ten-year-old pines growing on the other side of the valley. Garth watched it go and let out a long breath of total pleasure.

"You guys slacking again?" Kelsey crunched over the heap of fallen branches towards them, brushing pine needles from her spiky blonde hair. Hinu followed her quietly. "I think us girls should get all the good seats on the school trip."

The last saw stopped. Big feet trampled, and Max the Supervisor joined them. "Looking good, people," he said. "Another six years, and these little guys will be nice tall trees. No lower branches to make knots and get tangled. Just good straight timber."

Max moved away into a clear area, and started talking into his cellphone. The other four squatted down, backs against the smooth trunks. Water bottles and cookies appeared from packs. Danny had as many cookies as the rest of them put together. Garth never understood how his friend could eat so much and stay so skinny.

"Let's hope nobody cuts down the wrong ones this time," Max said, while they ate and drank. "There's a zone of pines just over the next ridge that were ready for thinning a couple of years back. I spent three or four days working through there and slapping red paint on the ones that needed cuttin' down. Then they sent in this two-man gang doing their first contract, and the idiots cut down every tree that *didn't* have red paint on it. That was their first Treecorp contract and their last Treecorp contract."

The four kids laughed. "Typical guys!" crowed Kelsey. "Useless!"

Over in the taller pines, where the crow had headed, a wind began to blow. Garth heard the scrape and thump of high branches knocking together.

Max stood and stretched. "Okay for another hour, team? Otherwise those pine branches will be growing up faster than we cut them down."

"Wonder how many Leah's gang have done?" Danny groaned twenty minutes later. "Two hundred and thirty-two!" he added.

A second team of Plains College kids was pruning a Treecorp zone about three miles away, with the other supervisor. Every tree was another step on the school trip to Hawaii. ("A bacteria-sized step!" said Kelsey after the first, blister-inducing day.) When they got back to camp tonight, they'd see which team had done the most. "Two hundred and thirty-three," murmured Hinu. Garth started sawing harder.

Pine was cool stuff to cut – straight grain – hardly any knots. Good timber to grow, too; every Plains College kid whose parents worked in the great forests around Kinross knew that. In those forests, millions of trees grew for twenty-five years, pruned and thinned and guarded against pests and fires till they were ready to be turned into boats and boxes, houses for people and houses for dogs. Trees in enormous zones that sprawled up ranges of hills, down deep valleys and across wide plateaus. So many of them that astronauts on the International Space Station could see the shape of the forest as they orbited far above.

The July afternoon was growing cool as they packed up. Two hundred and seventy-five pine saplings pruned. Sweet!

Garth flicked sawdust from his thick wool sweater and used the flap of his pack to wipe sap from his hooked saw. He picked up the first aid kit that he was looking after today and began making his way with the others back along the line of saplings to where Max had parked the SUV. In a few months, forestry workers with flame-throwers would come through here and burn off the slash – the heap of pruned branches on the ground – so it wouldn't become a fire hazard.

They walked carefully. Under the newly-cut branches, the ground was pitted with holes and lumpy with old roots. At the road, Garth turned and glanced back once more. In the ten minutes it had taken them to walk there, the July sun had crawled further down the sky, turning the gray tree trunks a glowing red.

Max steered the jolting SUV back along the gravel

road. Danny and Kelsey talked – mostly at the same time. Hinu gazed out of the window at the darkening rows of trees. Garth hoped Leah's team had gotten back to camp first and started cooking dinner.

The growl and grumble of heavy machinery grew ahead of them. Max slowed and pulled over beside a ditch of dark scummy water.

They'd come out of the tree zones and into an open area being prepared for replanting. Across a stretch of dipping ground the size of four football fields, around the bases of a line of towering power pylons, bulldozers and big earth-rippers ground their way. They crunched up the last dead branches from the pines felled there maybe five years ago, trailing spiked rollers that churned the soil ready for new trees to be planted, plowing and gouging the torn-up ground. Juniper, fern, and thistle waited to be smashed down by the steel blades.

Max had gotten out and was talking to a heavyset guy wearing the orange hard hat of a supervisor. The man was shaking his head. "Sorry, guys," said Kelsey. "We're not allowed to borrow their bulldozers for tomorrow's pruning." Danny grinned around another granola bar.

"Had a few idiots in the area." Max squeezed himself back into the driver's seat. "Guys on all-terrain vehicles – ATVs – using the forest for joy-rides. Treecorp's worried about their leaving cigarettes and stuff. If you see any, use your pruning saw on their tires. But you didn't hear me say that."

It was almost dark by the time they reached the forestry cabins in the grassy clearing. A locked shed marked

5

FIRE CREWS ONLY stood nearby. And – yes! – branches already glowed in the concrete fireplace: a fireplace built well clear of the cabins and surrounded by bare ground where no spark could catch and burn.

They'd needed special permission to use the fireplace, and the weird thing was that Garth's father was the Safety Officer they had to ask. "If anything goes wrong, then Garth is dog meat," he joked. At least, Garth hoped he was joking.

As they and Leah's team sat eating in one of the cozy cabins, Max and Leah talked about trees. They talked about a guy about a century or so back who'd wanted to plant a triangle-shaped forest with sides 90 miles long, because he thought creatures on other planets would see it. They discussed the way that cultivating pine trees meant native forests could be saved from felling. They even went on about how countries who'd cut down all the trees along their big rivers now suffered from terrible floods and landslides, while the water in those rivers was now so polluted, fish couldn't live in it.

"You two guys make sure that fire is completely out," Leah told Garth and Danny when the dishes were washed. Garth grunted. She didn't need to remind him; her safety lecture on the first night had described all the ways fires could start – lightning strikes; smoldering campfires; the sun shining through a dropped bottle. He took a shovel from under the cabin steps and headed out to spread dirt over the embers.

"I've got a better way," Danny muttered, swallowing his second after-dinner cookie. "We could –"

"No," came Max's voice from behind them. "I'll be checking later, so don't try to pee on it."

Also from behind them, Garth heard Kelsey sniggering.

TWO

Next morning, Garth stood outside his cabin and sucked in the pine-scented, sparkling-clean air. The wind blew, and he pulled his sweater sleeves down over his hands.

On every side of the clearing, green-black pine forest rose and dipped and stretched away. The early sun had turned the tops of one area a glowing gold. Around him, the world seemed to be standing still.

Garth stretched his arms above his head and realized his face was split in a huge, stupid grin. Heck, he'd work here even if it wasn't earning them anything for Hawaii. Kids who thought a forestry town was boring didn't have a clue. On this sort of morning, he could like everybody.

The door of the girls' cabin opened. Kelsey Brooking appeared, yawning and scratching her blonde spikes. Well, *almost* everybody, Garth decided.

The girl saw him and yawned again. "Seen Hinu? She's gone for a walk." As Garth shook his head, Kelsey went on. "Her ancestors used to live where the forest is now. She says she can still feel them here. Cool, huh?"

Garth didn't think it was cool. He thought it was pathetic. His father said Treecorp was always having to deal with Aboriginal people who wanted to hang onto their land because it was "spiritual" or something. Aboriginal people couldn't expect to live in the past and enjoy the present, he figured.

Garth's mom didn't agree. She liked the way they saw their land as sacred. Garth usually kept his mouth shut during the dinner-table arguments but, privately, he agreed with his dad.

"There she is." Kelsey pointed, and Garth saw a figure standing among the trees just beyond the clearing, face turned up as if she was listening to something. Silly – he started to think; then a door banged behind him and Danny emerged, scratching his head too. "When's breakfast?" he mumbled.

Kelsey glanced across at him. "Jeez, you look like dog food! With chunks."

"Yeah?" Danny yawned. "Yeah? Well, you look like *thrown-up* dog food. With chunks."

Garth grinned again. Nice to know that the others in the group were getting along so well.

At breakfast, Max told them about the time mice got into a forestry store cupboard and ate all the labels off the canned food. "So we just heated a couple of cans in boiling water every night and then opened them. We had hot spaghetti with hot peaches; hot corn with hot condensed milk – good stuff." The others shuddered. "Guys!" sneered Kelsey, and made gagging noises.

"You guys can cook tonight," Leah said, as her team

stuffed lunches and heavy work gloves into packs and picked up their hard hats. "You'll be back first; we're moving to a different zone as soon as we finish the one we're on."

Danny was still putting extra cookies into his jacket pockets when Max strode back from the middle of the clearing where he'd been talking on his cellphone and pausing to thump it occasionally. "They say it's gonna rain in a day or so. Let's get pruning, people."

Garth glanced up at a sky ribbed with thin gray clouds. He hated working in the rain. It dripped off branches into his eyes, down his neck and up his arms when he lifted them to saw.

Max and Danny headed around the back of the cabin to load the SUV. Garth wandered across the grass towards the nearest trees, kicking at dry needles, ducking under a spider web that glittered between two trunks. He hunched his shoulders as the wind blew harder. Ahead of him, a chickadee dodged and dived.

CRASH! Behind a tree on his left, something leaped, clattered, bounded away among the pine trunks. Garth yelled, felt his back prickle and his heart race.

Kelsey appeared from her hut. "What's wrong with you?"

"A deer. Took off suddenly. Scared the heck out of me." Garth stared into the shadows where the flying hooves had vanished. Nearby, the chickadee still circled. When he turned around, Hinu Katene stood beside Kelsey, watching him silently. No – not watching him. Watching the forest.

The SUV bumped past the highway-wide firebreaks that

sliced through the trees, and alongside a creek with a big yellow plastic-sealed dam across it: a water supply for firefighters – Leah had mentioned them in her safety lecture.

"We've had idiots swimming in there," Max grunted as they jolted by. "And would you believe that one of them even used the water to wash his stupid car?"

They came out into a small clear area. Ahead of them, above a zone of ten-year-old pines, rose the power pylons they'd seen yesterday. Max stopped, got out, reached for his cellphone. "Want to check something with Leah." He thumped the phone again. "Piece of crap!"

Beyond the trees in front, engines snarled. The bulldozers and rippers working. No, Garth realized. These engines sounded different. Higher and shriller, like—

Max tumbled back into the driver's seat, and slammed the door. "Idiots! Hang on, people!"

The four kids grabbed seatbacks and straps as the SUV shot forward. They tore into the pines and swung around a corner, sending the first aid kit tumbling into Garth's lap. Danny half-choked on a cookie. They crashed over a tree-root, roared past a blur of thick, corrugated trunks, and out into the big clearing where they'd paused yesterday afternoon.

The giant machines were gone. Instead, two ATVs zoomed across the rough, bare ground, skidding around the bases of pylons, shooting down into gullies and leaping up out of them, racing along the fringe of brushwood that swayed as they flashed past.

Max's face was furious. "If there were new trees there, those jerks would have killed them!" He was already half-way out of the SUV as it lurched to a stop beside the scummy ditch, striding across the uneven ground, yelling and shaking his fist.

The two riders – Garth saw they were young; one with a helmet, one with dark hair blowing – roared on. Then the helmeted one saw them. He braked suddenly and began shouting to his friend.

The other guy didn't hear him. The ATV engines, plus the wind now whipping across the clearing, sending dust flying and stinging, drowned out Max's yells, too. The second ATV rocked around a pylon and almost into the thicket, swerving so that two of its wheels tilted off the ground.

Then the dark-haired rider also saw them. Next minute, both guys were shouting to each other across the clearing. The helmeted rider jabbed a finger at the gravel road. The other guy accelerated, skidded sideways, then began heading towards it, angling to keep away from Max, who was now running across a gully towards him.

The dark-haired rider veered, jolting round a clump of brush. As the guy jerked around to see where Max was, the ATV's front wheels crashed into a half-sunken log. The vehicle swung up, fat rear wheels aiming at the sky. Almost in slow motion, it seemed, the rider went sprawling on the ground, while the ATV somersaulted end over end into the thicket.

Everything happened so quickly that – for a second – Garth couldn't breathe. Then he heard Kelsey scream. He saw branches splinter as the heavy bike crashed into them, glimpsed something round and metal fly in the air, heard the crashing and crunching.

The guy in the helmet began climbing off his ATV. The other rider scrambled up, stared at Max, still stumbling and shouting towards him, then took off for the undamaged bike.

Garth pushed open his door. "He's getting—" He stopped. The helmeted rider was running, too. Running away from his undamaged ATV, towards the one lying upside-down in the brush. He won't be able to get it going in time, Garth knew. Not before Max reached him.

Then Garth saw it, too. The flickering in the dry growth where the ATV had landed. The orange flare and sudden puff of smoke. The brush was on fire.

All four kids wrenched their way out of the SUV. Garth and Danny began charging towards the smoke rising on the far side of the clearing, then swung round as someone yelled, "Take these!" Hinu was pulling shovels from the back. Garth snatched one and took off again. It was the first time he'd heard Hinu raise her voice.

She was staring past them at the two ATV riders, who had reached one another in the middle of the smashed ground. The helmeted one pointed at the flames. The other shook his head and pulled away, starting towards the ATV that still stood with its engine running.

A clump of grass seemed to jerk suddenly, and orange fire ran up it. The helmeted guy sprinted towards the blaze. He reached it, began grabbing handfuls of dirt and chucking them on the flames, stamping on the ones nearest to him. His friend stood, yelling at him. A gust of wind sent the black smoke swirling.

The fire wasn't too big, Garth saw as he and the others

came hurrying up. Their shovels could smother it. Luckily the dirt around was already churned up.

Ahead of him, Danny shouldered past the ATV rider, plunged his shovel into the ground, slung earth and stones on to the orange glow. The rider had snatched off his helmet and was using it to scoop up dirt, too. Green eyes stared from a skinny face.

I've seen him somewhere, Garth thought. Hinu arrived, began gasping something to the boy, and started shoveling, as well.

"Chuck it at the base of the flames!" Max yelled. His big fist grabbed the guy's shoulder. "You idiot! You've got oatmeal for brains, son. See what you've done!"

It wasn't he who…Garth thought, as he sent another shovelful of dirt at the fire. Beside him, Danny and Kelsey and Hinu dug and flung. The flames had already stopped on the side nearest them. If the wind didn't—

The growl of an engine snapped his up. The other rider, the dark-haired one, was on the undamaged ATV, bucking and bouncing towards the road. He reached it, glanced back once, then accelerated away, vanishing between the pines.

For three seconds maybe, the other six stood, shovels and bike helmet in hand, staring after him.

Then behind them, the ATV's gas tank exploded.

THREE

It went up with a *WHOOMMPFF!* and a blast of hot air that pulled at Garth's clothes. As the shock wave blew flames and smoke sideways, he glimpsed the broken shape of the ATV lying in the charred brush. Three yards away, a gas tank cap glinted on the ground. Garth recognized the metal disc he'd seen spinning through the air just moments before.

He cringed as fire and heat rained down, just past were he stood. Something bit the back of his wrist above his work glove and clung there, stinging and searing. Garth yelped and slapped his other glove down over the burning drop of fuel.

A shriek sounded behind him. Kelsey was reeling, clawing at her spiky blonde hair. Her head was on fire.

Garth dived for her, but Hinu got there first. She knocked the screaming girl to the ground, sprawling on top of her, smothering the spitting flames. Max left the ATV rider and reached them in two steps. As Hinu rolled away, the supervisor dropped beside Kelsey, cupping her head in his big hands. The guy with the helmet stared. He was about their age, with a bony jaw and bristly brown stubble on his head. I know him, Garth thought again.

"You're okay." Max spoke calmly to Kelsey. "You're okay. A few scorch marks, but your hair stopped it. Keep your hard hat on from now on." He turned to where the others stood panting. "All of you, keep them on. This is what they're meant for."

The supervisor helped Kelsey up. She felt her head cautiously, groaned at the burned, acrid-smelling crisps of hair in her hand. "Jeez, that cost me sixty bucks at Hair Today!"

The wind blew again. Danny yelled and pointed. They whirled to see the flames rear up in the undergrowth, surging away from the brush. A juniper bush snapped and crackled, as the berrylike cones popped open. The fire covered an area as big as a house now. Their shovels weren't going to stop it. Wind gusted from a different direction, and smoke blew in their faces, making them cough and sputter.

"Get back to the truck!" Max told them. "Kelsey needs water on that scorched head. We gotta call the fire crews." He glared at the ATV rider. "You come with us, son. You're in pretty big trouble."

The six of them began hurrying across the bare, rutted ground. Behind them, Garth heard the fire crack and surge again as wind caught it. He glanced a look back. It was moving towards the pines.

Danny and Garth chucked their shovels into the back of the SUV, among the pruning saws and ropes and other gear. Garth was sweating under his thick wool sweater, but already he could feel his back cooling off as they stood in the shade of the trees. He remembered the weather forecast. Jeez, he wished it *would* rain now!

Hinu used her hard hat to scoop dirty, brown water from the roadside ditch. "Close your eyes!" she ordered, and poured it over Kelsey's bent head.

The other girl squealed. "It's freezing!" She squealed again as another hatful poured over her singed, soaked, shapeless hair. She wiped her face and stared at her hand. "And it's gross!"

"Keep doing that," grunted Max, reaching for his cellphone. "Another half a dozen lots." As he headed towards open ground, pausing to thump the phone, Garth and Danny plunged their own plastic hats into the ditch, and poured them over Kelsey's head. She swore and sputtered. The eyes of the two boys met, and Garth felt a half-snicker twist his mouth. I've always wanted to do this to Kelsey Brooking, he thought.

He glanced again at the girl's charred, blackened hair. Do I dare tell her she's really a *hot* chick now? he thought. Nah, not if I want to keep my teeth. The guy from the ATV stood watching, still holding his helmet, Hinu beside him. Beyond the cleared ground, orange tongues flickered and spread.

Max stamped back to them, face tight. "Stupid phone's shot!"

"They'll see the smoke, won't they?" asked Danny.

"They need details as soon as possible – size, direction, what's burning." Max stood for a second, swore as another juniper bush blazed and crackled.

"Will they send a chopper to put it out?" Garth asked.

The supervisor shook his head. "Too close to the pylons. They'll need ground crews." He glared once more at the twisting thread of fire advancing towards the trees. Hinu was murmuring to the ATV rider. Hey, Garth realized. They—

Max's voice interrupted him. "Get in the truck, everyone. We'll find Leah's team, use her phone."

They piled into the SUV. The guy hesitated, then lurched in after Danny as Max shoved him. Garth watched the jerking flames as the truck roared off down the road. A black, filthy line of burned brush already showed behind them. Smoke from it circled and rose towards the sky. The day was smeared and fouled.

"It's like the evil spirits" Hinu spoke quietly from the back, where Kelsey was dragging off her wet sweater and scrabbling for another. "There's always been an evil spirit in the river, waiting to attack this land."

Fear surged in Garth. "Try making sense!" he snarled. Danny, another cookie already in his hand, shot a sideways glance at him.

The SUV dashed across the cleared ground and through a grouping of small pines like the ones they'd pruned yesterday. The fire was behind them now, and the air was clean and sharp, except for the smoky smell of their clothes, and the stink of Kelsey's burned hair.

"The pines won't burn, will they?" The blonde girl's voice sounded shaky.

Max wrenched at the steering wheel. They skidded around a bend, gravel flying, and past a taller dead tree that stood by the road, one too bent and twisted to be worth cutting. "There's slash lying on the ground in that zone. Pruned stuff – it'll be dry now. They've been getting ready to do a controlled burn of it. If the fire gets in it, it'll be like kindling." Another bend; another skid that sent them grabbing at the seats. "Then we'll have a big one. Big enough to make its own wind."

Garth tried to picture it. Instead his mind saw the chickadees and the crow. And that deer.

The SUV raced out of the small pines, across a firebreak and into a block of taller trees Suddenly, cool green light was all around them.

Garth twisted round to see if there was somehow any sign of the fire behind. Instead, he found himself staring at Kelsey. She was crying silently. Tears curved down her cheeks, still filthy from the ditch water. Hinu had an arm around her shoulder and was murmuring to her. Hinu's eyes met Garth's, and he looked away.

"What's your name?" Garth jerked, then realized Max was talking to the ATV rider. He'd almost forgotten the guy, squeezed in on the far side of Danny.

There was no reply. Then everyone jumped as Max yelled. "What's your *name!*"

"Isaac Belton." The voice was low and flat.

"And who's your friend – the brave one who ran away?"

The ATV guy was silent again for a second. Then, "He can tell you."

"Don't—" Hinu began, and suddenly Garth knew where he'd seen the guy before.

The truck tore over a rut in the gravel road, and he

felt his head whack into the roof. Max slammed a hand down on the steering wheel, and the horn gave a stupid *toot*. "Don't you know anything about forests? Don't you realize this is exactly why we try to stop morons like you from coming in? You dumb—"

Isaac Belton spoke, louder this time. "Yeah, I know about forests. My old man worked here half his life – till a tree fell on him, smashed him inside his bulldozer."

He goes out with Hinu, Garth was thinking as the other boy spoke. Used to, anyway. I've seen them at the movies in Kinross. Heck, I thought she had better taste.

The engine howled as Max chopped down a gear. Garth clung to the seatback in front as the supervisor twisted the wheel, and the SUV nearly slid off the road, dirt hurtling into the air. Next moment, they were jolting and bucking down a firebreak.

The fifty-yard wide belt of bare ground stretched ahead of them. The forest was crisscrossed with firebreaks: They were the gaps to stop flames spreading from one zone of trees to another, the emergency routes along which crews would hurry to fight any blaze.

Max fought the wheel as the SUV tore along, slipping and sliding on the ungraded surface. There was a half-shout from several of the kids as they skidded sideways for a moment. Then, as Max accelerated and they roared forward again, Garth caught a it – a small, ugly stain of smoke rising into the sky behind them.

On either side, the rows of pine trunks flashed past. A bump that lifted Garth right off his seat, another wrench at the wheel, and they went hurtling down a different road that dropped into a valley. Garth saw whatsisname – Isaac

– clinging to a strap on the other side of Danny. His face had no expression.

They skidded around yet another bend, scraped a clay bank and swung off the road onto a stretch of thin grass flecked with orange pine needles. Max braked to a ground-tearing halt, and next second they were tumbling from the truck.

Around them, the forest sprawled dark and empty. Fresh wheel marks curved across the stretch of grass ahead. There was no sign of Leah and her team.

FOUR

They stood there in the gray-green light that slanted through the pines. Above them, a cool wind breathed through the treetops. Trunks creaked; high branches scraped.

Max tried his cellphone again, shook it and shoved it back into his pocket. "Okay, listen up. They could all have gone on to their next job, like Leah said. But we have to check. We're going to walk in a few hundred yards, see if they're still working in there. Kelsey, you stay with the truck. Blow the horn if anyone turns up. The rest of you, spread out in a line and start calling. Keep your hard hats on, and make sure you can see the people on either side of you." He swung toward Isaac. "Wear your motorcycle helmet – not that you've got an actual brain to protect. And don't even think about running away, or I swear I'll—"

The stubble-headed kid glared back. "I'm not going anywhere." Hinu opened her mouth then closed it again.

Max eyeballed him for another second, then turned to the others, "Come on. And keep shouting for them."

The fuel burn on the back of Garth's wrist stung again as they started towards the trees. He'd forgotten it during the crazy ride in the SUV; he'd had more important things to do – like praying they stayed on the road. Now, as they moved into the pines and the temperature dropped, he took off his glove and let the cool air soothe it.

Hinu walked on one side of him, fifteen yards away. "Leah?" she called. Away to Garth's left, Danny yelled, too. "Leah? Anyone there?" No reply.

Isaac was between Garth and Danny. He wore jeans and boots, jacket, leather gloves. He almost looked like a forestry worker, except for the black motorcycle helmet.

Garth thought of what the boy had said about his father. A tree…Was his dad dead? People still died in forestry work: even Garth's father, who loved the life so much, often spoke of how dangerous it was. Trees twisted as they fell; big branches dropped like spears from high above; chainsaws snapped suddenly; trucks capsized. And then there was fire. Garth glanced up through the column of trees again. No sign of any smoke. No sign of rain, either, just those wispy, gray clouds.

"Leah?" Hinu called again. Garth glanced at her, then at Isaac. Bet she feels pretty sick right now, he thought. Serves her – He stopped, shook himself, yelled "Leah?" too. Still nothing.

"Hey?" Isaac was speaking to him. "Who're we looking for?"

"The other supervisor. She had a team working somewhere around here. Max wants to find them and use her phone."

Isaac nodded. "Leah?" he called. Then louder. "Leah?"

They moved on between the trees. This zone was too tall for pruning; Leah's team must have been further in. The branches twenty yards up rubbed against one another once more as the wind gusted. The tops sighed like waves. Trees are so...so calm, Garth thought; even when they're moving. They quiet you down just by being near them.

Isaac was staring upwards, too. He saw Garth watching. "Big ones, huh? My old man said they're worth about seven-hundred bucks each."

"*Said*" did that mean his father was no longer...? Then Garth saw light ahead. They were nearing the end of the big trees; on the other side of a thin firebreak stood the three-year-old pines where Leah's gang must have been working. Through the avenues of thin trunks, Garth could see freshly cut branches lying on the ground. Nobody was there.

Max swore under his breath. He stood for a moment looking up and down the firebreak. "Come on. Back to the truck."

Beside the SUV, Max shook, thumped, and swore at his cellphone again. The others stood, smacking gloved hands together in the chill air.

"Pity there aren't more animals in the forest," Danny said suddenly, around a mouthful of granola bar.

Kelsey stared at him. "What? Like snakes and birds and spiders?"

"Nah. Other stuff you read about but don't get to see. I dunno."

Garth realized his friend was talking to hide his nervousness; one corner of his mouth twitched. Kelsey was edgy too, running a hand through her scorched hair, glancing up at the sky. Hinu stood beside her, looking into the trees. She hadn't spoken to Isaac again; had hardly looked at him. I guess she *does* have better taste after all, Garth decided.

He stared up. No smoke. Maybe the fire had stopped before it reached those pines. Maybe there hadn't been time for the slash to start burning.

Isaac glanced at the filthy, matted mess of Kelsey's hair. "Sorry," he mumbled.

The girl gave him a look that seemed likely to make *his* hair catch fire. "Thanks a bunch. Only a guy could say something that useless."

Isaac's bony jaw tightened. Then Danny spoke. "Wind's changing."

Yeah, Garth realized. The pines were bending in a different direction, bowing, lifting, bowing again as the wind poured through them. Yeah, that could stop the fire before it hit the trees.

Max whistled to them from the SUV. He didn't look happy. "We're heading back."

There's teams of forest firefighters all over the region that Treecorp can call in, Garth reminded himself as the SUV wound back up the hill. They've got choppers to spray chemicals on fires – all kinds of stuff. They might even decide to just let it burn itself out. His dad had told him that happened sometimes, though Garth knew from the way he said it that he hated letting *any* trees burn.

They swung off the road and back along the firebreak. Max was still driving fast, but not like a maniac any longer. Garth glimpsed something like a white metal mailbox inside a wire enclosure at the firebreak's edge: a remote control weather station. Every day dozens of them fed data on temperature, wind, humidity and ground conditions to a computer at Treecorp headquarters.

His head jerked around suddenly. Max was stopping. What —?

The supervisor turned in his seat to look at them. "Should have told you what I'm doing. Leah's probably taken her team to the next job, like she said. It's miles away. So we're heading back to see what's happened to the fire. It's our job, since we saw it first. Soon as we can report to someone, we're out of here."

He paused. Five grimy faces stared back at him. "We stick together from now on, remember? Nobody goes off by themselves. Nobody."

His gaze shifted to Isaac. "Your dad Cliff Sinclair?"

"Yeah." The boy's green eyes met Max's. "I use my mom's name now."

Max said nothing. The SUV revved and moved on again. On either side of the firebreak, the trees bent and lifted in the wind. There was still no smoke. Garth felt better with every minute that passed.

They churned off the firebreak, back onto the gravel road and through the zone of taller trees. Max hauled at the wheel, whacked the gear lever up or down, floored the accelerator.

Behind him, the five kids sat silent. Hawaii is going to be boring after this, Garth decided. Am I gonna have some stories to tell the kids back at school! Hey, he thought then, I hope none of the trees we pruned get burned. They might not pay us for them!

The next firebreak came into view, with the stand of smaller pines beyond. As they rushed out into the open, a flicker made Garth glance sideways. A crow. A second one, then a couple of chickadees, flying after it, all heading in the opposite direction of the SUV. He'd seen this before, small birds chasing much bigger ones away from their nests. Amazing, really.

They plunged into the young pines, past the twisted dead tree, and suddenly the light went dull. Garth peered ahead, and relief washed over him. Clouds. Low clouds, right down over the trees. It was going to rain. The forest would be all right.

Then, as Max hit the brakes, he realized it was smoke.

FIVE

The SUV skidded to a halt. The six of them sat silently, gaping through the windshield.

Blue-gray coils of smoke flowed through the pine tops, eddying as the wind tugged at them. For another moment, Garth tried to tell himself it was mist, wreathing in the trees the way it did on cold mornings, or else the steam that rose from the trunks as the sun warmed them. No, it was smoke. The wind had changed; the fire had moved in another direction. How big was it now? What was it burning?

Max spoke quietly. "All right. Smoke's a signal, and it's a danger. Smoke can blind you or choke you so you can't think properly. If you've got a handkerchief or a scarf, keep it ready to put over your face. Anyone wearing contact lenses? You'll need to take them out."

Nobody answered. "I'm going to go forward – try and check the fire status. I can turn in a couple of seconds on this road, so it shouldn't be a problem. Then we're leaving – fast. You guys can get out and wait here till I come back, if you want."

Again there was silence. None of them wanted to be

left alone, Garth knew. Somehow it wasn't so scary in the truck. He glanced at the others. Danny opened his mouth, then shut it – without even putting any food in it. Kelsey swatted at her mess of hair. Hinu and Isaac sat still. Hope she picks her boyfriends more carefully from now on, Garth thought.

They all jumped as a rush of wind sent the slender pines rubbing against one another. Pines were hard to blow over because of the way they gave with the wind, but there'd been storms in this forest that flattened entire zones, Garth's dad had told him. Jeez, there better not be anything like that today.

The SUV crept forward. Smoke formed, shredded, flowed closer. Garth could smell it now, thin and sour. Sinister somehow: he thought of the evil spirit Hinu had mentioned. Stupid. He felt angry suddenly at the way his mom kept sticking up for Aboriginal feelings about the land. His dad was right: treating a place like it was full of spirits or stuff wouldn't help anyone now.

They rounded a curve. A bank of clay studded with old tree roots rose on one side. The smoke was getting lower. Then Garth jerked and stared. A work team was hurrying out of the forest ahead.

He glimpsed the movement first, then the orange jackets and yellow hard hats. Had Leah—? A second later, his throat went tight. It wasn't people. It was flames.

Max was already bringing the SUV to a halt, reversing in a three-point turn between the ditches that flanked the road. "Low Vigor Surface Fire," Garth heard him mutter. "No spotting."

Leah had used the same names in her safety lecture. Forest fires came in three types, she'd told them: Ground Fires that spread slowly, burning only leaves and litter; Surface Fires that fed on slash and scorched a few pines as they passed; Crown Fires where the whole tree burned.

It was Crown Fires that every forestry worker feared, blazes where entire pines flamed like torches, fire jumping across their tops faster than a person could run. And it was Crown Fires that sent burning needles and twigs flying on the wind to start other fires spotting ahead of them, cutting firefighters off.

The wind whipped as the SUV pulled out of its turn to face back the way they'd come. Behind them now, tongues of orange licked along the ground, circling trunks, sending hot tongues knee-high as twigs and fallen branches caught. The flames stopped as another wind gust blew them back on themselves, flared again and came on. Smoke crept ahead of the flames. They were moving no faster than walking speed, but Garth's heart thumped as he watched.

The truck's door banged as Max jumped out, cellphone in hand. Garth's anger surged. He saw Danny's mouth twitch again. "Why's he—?" Then they realized the phone was working, and the supervisor was shouting into it, staggering as the wind smacked at him. "Zone seventeen…" Garth heard. "Low Vigor…Has Leah—?" Max stopped, banged the phone, swore, then tumbled back into the SUV.

"I think Leah's team is out," he grunted as they accelerated away from the creeping orange line behind them. "And so are we." He glanced into the rear-view mirror at Isaac. "A lot of people want to talk to you, son. And your gutless friend."

Whew! Garth thought, as they barreled round a corner and the fire vanished from sight. Now the fire crews could take over. Yeah, he was certainly going to have some stories to impress kids at school. Maybe he'd get his buddies to tell Kelsey to keep her hair the way it was – if they really wanted to end up in the emergency room.

The end of the young pine zone was ahead. Wind rocked the truck; it swerved as Max yanked at the wheel. And at the forest edge in front of them, the dead tree swayed, swung back, swayed forward again as the wind slammed at it, and came crashing down, slowly and almost gracefully, onto the road. Branches splintered. The trunk bounced a couple of times, then lay still, while twigs pattered down around it. The road was blocked.

They pulled themselves out of the truck and stared, unable to believe what they were seeing. Garth was sweating again, not from effort this time. A gust of cold air whipped past, and he felt the goose-bumps rise on his skin. Another couple of birds skimmed by, away from the slowly following flames. The pines lashed in the wind as if they were trying to escape as well.

Danny and Kelsey began hauling at the fallen tree, heaving and wrenching. The trunk didn't even shake. Garth glanced at the narrow, deep ditches on either side of the road. No way could the SUV get around there.

"Can't we cut through it?" Danny's mouth kept twitching. Blood showed on his knuckles where he'd scraped them on the tree trunk.

"Ram it!" urged Kelsey. "Push it with the truck!"

Max shook his head. Isaac watched, gripping his motorcycle helmet. Three...four hundred yards behind them, the curtain of smoke climbed and crawled. Garth glimpsed a flash of orange, like an eye watching them. Hinu gazed at it, too.

"Can we stay in the SUV?" Danny was asking now. "Keep the windows up so the smoke can't get us? The fire will go past us if we're on the road, won't it?"

"Can't my friend." Max's voice was gentle, and Garth understood that he'd sensed the panic growing around him. "The gas tank could turn into a bomb – you've already seen that happen. And if the truck heats up, all the plastic and vinyl gives off poisonous fumes. Vehicles are a death-trap."

He looked behind him, and Garth followed his gaze. Half-a-dozen tongues of fire showed now. One flared up as it reached a patch of slash or needles.

"We're gonna walk out," Max said. The others stared at him. "Grab your packs. Make sure you've got your gloves and hard hats. Kelsey, get rid of that parka and take the old wool jacket from the truck. Anyone else wearing synthetics? Whatever you do, don't let them near any flames.They'll start pouring out hydrogen cyanide if they burn. You breathe that, and you'll be dead in a couple of minutes. Come on, now – move!"

Garth hauled his pack out of the SUV, hesitated, then stuffed the first aid kit into it. He tried to breathe deep and stay calm. On the sixth or seventh breath, he smelled the acrid tang of smoke. Back behind them, the orange-red spots had joined into a thin line. The creaking, swaying pines drowned out any sound from the flames.

"Danny, Garth. You – Isaac. Take a shovel each. It's all right, people. We're gonna be okay. We stick together; we walk quickly but we don't run. We'll head for that big firebreak – the one we came along, remember? We'll get into the middle, use the gear to make ourselves a nice safe area, and we'll be fine. Let's go."

They scrambled over the splintered tree-trunk, knots catching at their packs and clothes. Isaac slid across like a lizard, and held out a hand to Kelsey as she struggled after him. The girl knocked it away.

On the other side, Garth tucked the short-handled shovel under the outside straps of his pack, while Danny and Hinu climbed over the fallen pine. It was the same shovel he'd used to try and smother the flames around the ATV...what, just forty minutes ago?

A distant *crack!* made him turn and look. Back in the line of flames, a young pine was burning. Fire spread upwards, like the flag of an army coming after them.

"Okay?" Max called, and they started off. Every step takes us further ahead of the fire, Garth told himself. Max is right – we just have to reach that firebreak and we're okay.

From Leah's talk just three nights ago, a word flickered into his mind: *FEAR*. The thing to do when a fire was obviously out of control: *Forget Everything And Run*. At least they weren't running. Yet.

SIX

They reeled as another wind-gust whacked them. While he strode on, Garth tried to remember what was in his pack. Sandwiches, a couple of apples, water bottle, parka. The first aid kit.

He pictured the extra cookies and stuff crammed into Danny's pack, turned his head sideways and told his friend, "We'll be all right in the firebreak, mate. Choppers will probably see us there."

Danny's mouth still trembled. He was trying not to break into a run. "Yeah. Sorry I started to lose it back there, okay?"

Garth thumped him on the shoulder as they hurried around a bend. The wind rushed again, and Hinu staggered. Garth grabbed her elbow; it felt warm and slender. Brown eyes, a tiny scar underneath one, stared into his for a moment, then the girl pushed on.

They were covering ground, no doubt about that. Already, the smoke and ugly creep of fire was further behind. Max strode in front, eyes scanning ahead and to the sides, murmuring to Kelsey, who kept breaking into a trot to keep up with him. Isaac came next, long legs scissoring along. He'd taken a bag from the truck to put the shovel in, and tied a bit of twine for a sling over his shoulder. Sensible – if you could use "sensible" for the guy who'd started this. Okay, *partly* started it; his no-brain friend was the real culprit. At least Isaac had tried to do something about it.

Garth gazed around, like Max. On one side of the road, forest zones angled down towards the gorge of the Pine River, less than a mile or so away. On the other, they rose to a line of short hills, with more valleys and hills beyond. The town of Kinross and his home were over there somewhere, on the far side of the main road, fifteen miles away. Garth couldn't figure out the exact direction. News of the fire had probably reached his father in Treecorp's headquarters by now. He wondered if his mother had seen the smoke. Would she guess what it meant?

They came puffing out into the sudden light and emptiness of the small firebreak. Suddenly, the wind whipped at them. The same thin ribs of cloud trekked overhead.

"This where – we're stopping?" Kelsey gasped.

Max shook his head. The big man didn't seem to be breathing any harder. "Too narrow. Smoke could reach us here. Sparks and heat, too. This is mainly an access strip. We go through the next zone, then we reach the big break. Come on, people. We're doing fine."

They set off along the road, towards where it pointed into the shadows between the next tall pines. Garth glanced back again, then stopped. He couldn't see any flames, but the smoke was different, somehow – thicker at one end. Was the wind blowing it all in that direction? Had—?

"Hey!" Max's yell made him jerk. The others were already twenty yards ahead. They'd stopped and were staring back at him. "Come on!" the supervisor yelled. "What the heck are ya doing?"

Garth broke into a jog to catch up. Kelsey gave him a look, muttered something about "useless males," then turned and hurried on. Garth stayed at the back, trying to figure out how that smoke had looked.

For another ten...twelve minutes, they strode along in silence. The rhythm of their marching started to relax Garth. The tall cool trees, bowing and straightening in the wind, their avenues of dark green and gray passing beside him, made the fire seem far away.

Ahead of him, Hinu walked beside Isaac, talking to him. Garth couldn't hear her words, but the anger in them was clear. The skinny boy said nothing. After a bit, Hinu dropped back to be with Kelsey. Isaac walked on, staring at the ground.

Garth snatched another look back. Just a couple of smoke stains marked the sky. The air around was scented with pine resin. Garth filled his lungs, let it out as he moved on, breathed in again. "Good stuff, man," he told Danny. His friend gave him a tight grin.

How far to the big firebreak? They'd taken just three or four minutes to tear through this zone in the SUV that first time, but Max must have been doing fifty to sixty miles an hour on the rutted road. So that meant—

"About thirty minutes to the break!" the supervisor

called, as if he'd been reading Garth's mind. "Hang in there, people. We're gonna be okay!"

Kelsey gave a half-gasp, half-grunt, and ploughed on, hard hat bouncing on her charred, filthy hair. Danny wiped his grimy face. His companions pushed forward.

The SUV...Garth pictured it back on the road by the fallen tree, fire advancing on it, maybe all around it now. Would it be destroyed? A forest fire could melt steel if it burned hot enough. This was going to cost Treecorp a lot. He wouldn't want to be Isaac, or that spineless friend of his.

Wind roared in the treetops over to his right. Was it coming from a different angle again? Hard to tell with the pines all around. All down the rows of gray columns, he could hear branches knocking.

Seven hundred dollars for a tree, Isaac had said. Yeah, that was about right. And every tree this fire destroyed made a difference to the environment. Every tree, his dad had told him, was like a giant cleaner, sucking carbon dioxide out of the air through its needles, pumping oxygen back in. Trees and humans needed one another to survive.

Ahead of him, Kelsey's head was down, but she struggled on. Hinu was breathing hard but looked okay. The four guys loped along. Danny seemed calmer. The firebreak couldn't be far now, and choppers would probably be watching it. Fifteen minutes, maybe, and they'd be there.

Over to Garth's right again, the big trunks flailed and swung as a gust battered through. Deep inside the zone, a couple of them smashed together with a bang that made Garth turn and look.

As he watched, far down in the lines of lofty gray shapes, a treetop exploded in flame.

The others had stopped in mid-stride, and were staring, too. Max's mouth was a thin line. Shock and disbelief gripped Kelsey's and Danny's faces.

That thick smoke, Garth understood. The wind had changed, all right. The fire was being blown in a curve around and at them from the side. He jumped as another burst of orange-red appeared in the trees. His mouth felt thick; his guts were heavy. Jeez, what was happening in there?

Max spoke, tight but calm. "We've got a problem, people. It's into the big growth and it's becoming a Crown Fire. Looks like it'll reach this road before we make the firebreak."

A whimpering noise from Danny. Isaac jerked his head towards the side of the road. "Can we get in the ditches? They're deep, and there's water in them."

Max shook his head. "You'll still have to breathe. When that fire gets here, you'll be sucking in superheated air. It'll burn your lungs. Plus there's the radiant heat; it'll get you even if the flames don't."

The Supervisor stared into the pines on the other side of the road, away from the fire. "We're heading into that zone. We'll make for the Pine River."

"It's in a huge gorge!" Kelsey half-screamed, half-shouted. She shook her head angrily; made herself speak more quietly. "There's cliffs. You can't get down them."

"There's a little gully you can climb down." Other heads swung as Hinu spoke, quietly as ever. "My grandfather took me there once. It's a special place. Some of *his* grandfather's people escaped down it when they were being attacked."

Jeez! Garth yelled silently as they all stared at the girl. Never mind the stories about the old days. Just *get* us there!

They scrambled across the roadside ditch, Kelsey swearing as she slipped and came up with one leg soaked to the knee. They stumbled through the band of old fallen logs and waist-high weeds into the pines. The trees didn't feel calm any longer. They swung and bent, almost as if they knew what was coming for them.

Sweating, panting, stumbling on the rough ground, the six of them hurried down the row ahead. They were jogging now. This is *FEAR*, all right, Garth admitted to himself. Hinu was in front, Max at the rear. "Keep together!" the supervisor called once again.

Kelsey was struggling again, bent forward under her pack. Isaac stuck out a hand and began yanking it off her shoulders. "Give it to me, you stupid chick!" he snarled, as she tried to twist away. Kelsey glared, raised her arms so he could pull off the pack, and crashed on. Man, Garth found himself thinking; he's braver than me!

A patchy carpet of dry pine needles stretched underfoot. There was no slash to start burning in here, but Garth knew that a Crown Fire didn't need that. It would leap from treetop to treetop in great bounds.

He could smell smoke again. In the air? On their clothes? How close was the blaze behind them now? The road would slow it for a bit, surely.

A banging burst out, straight above. Garth hunched in terror. The fire had caught them.

Then he realized. It was a chopper, hidden by the trees. No way could it see them in here. If only they'd stayed by the road. He didn't dare look at Max. He plunged on with the rest. The burn on his wrist had begun stinging again.

They lurched over tree roots, slipped on needles and fallen pine cones. Garth wouldn't let himself look back. The ground was definitely sloping downward now. How long before—?

So suddenly that he heard Danny call out, they were in the open. The pines ended. A huge sweep of sky arced over them. Twenty yards ahead, the plateau ended in a cliff that plunged straight down to the Pine River churning way below. On the far side, the dark zones of pines marched on.

Hinu pointed. "Over there." Garth saw it. A little gully, like a notch in the lip of the gorge, slanting down towards the river. It was steep and narrow, but there was undergrowth, brush, and a few stunted little self-sown pines dotted down it. Plenty of handholds. They could get down there and across the river. Across to safety.

SEVEN

"Watch where you're going," Max urged as the six of them began climbing over fallen branches, scrambling around stump-holes towards the top of the gully. "Anyone breaks an ankle, we're in real trouble." He pushed through to the front. "You been down here before, Hinu?"

The dark-haired girl shook her head. "Grandpa wouldn't let me. He said too many terrible things happened in this place."

Oh, please! Garth thought again. Let's move! Beside him, Danny clasped and unclasped his gloved hands. Kelsey and Isaac spoke at the same time. "He'd want you to now...It'll help other people escape." They glared at each other. Isaac glanced at Hinu, then looked away.

Hinu said nothing for a moment. Then she pointed. "He said there was a way down from here."

"Here" was a boulder the size of a table, sunk in the ground at the gully's rim, dappled with lichen and moss. There were patterns carved on it, Garth noticed suddenly: circles and spirals. Or was it just the grain of the rock? Beside it, a

41

line like the ghost of a track angled sharply down, towards a little pine sapling, across to a clump of ferns, then on and down even more steeply.

Max stood, eyes searching the half-ravine below. "Me first. Face the slope when it's your turn. If you start to slip, spread your arms out and grab anything you can. Leave a couple of body-lengths between you and the person below, so you're not kicking stones in their face." He turned to Isaac. "Keep your motorcycle helmet on. And the rest of you – make sure your hard hats are fastened tight."

In single file, handhold by handhold, kicking their feet into the thin dirt or jamming them between roots, they started down. Kelsey followed Max, scorched ends of hair poking out from under her yellow hard hat. Then Danny, looking better now he was doing something.

Max worked his way down to another, smaller boulder and crouched gripping it, telling Kelsey and Danny where to put hands and feet. Beneath him, the gully narrowed and turned at an angle. Garth couldn't see its bottom half, but there below was the Pine, rushing down its rock-choked bed. On the far side curved a little comma of sandy bank strewn with driftwood. Beyond that, reeds and rough grass for maybe thirty yards, then a zone of big, fifteen-year-old pines. They'd be safe there. The fire couldn't climb down cliffs and cross a river.

Isaac had started down now, still wearing Kelsey's pack and the sack with the shovel in it. His black helmet made him look like some mountaineering alien. He moved steadily, arms and legs flowing over the ground. Garth glanced at Hinu, then back at the sky above the zone they'd just run through. His back stiffened, and he stared harder. Smoke – thin, rising and blowing away, merging with the dirty-gray ribs of cloud. He turned quickly and began edging into the gully.

It was scary but not impossible. The others had already kicked out a route as they crept downwards. There were plenty of handholds; he just had to watch where he was going.

The big boulder. The little pine. Down and across to the fern, its roots anchored in the sloping rock. Straight down then, the toes of his boots scraping as he went, to another sturdy self-sown pine. The second boulder, with a ledge at the bottom where he could brace his feet. Below him, Max inched downwards, still calling instructions to Kelsey and Danny. The trees above boomed as wind thundered through them, but here in the valley they were sheltered, thank God.

He glanced up. Hinu was edging down, face towards the slope. Her lips moved. She...she was praying or something? Come on, Garth thought. It's not that bad!

As she reached the sapling above him, he realized she was murmuring in her native language, her words rising and falling, almost chanting.

Then he heard the other voices. Seemed to hear them, anyway. Like something glimpsed from the corner of his eye, they were there and not there. Calling in the same words Hinu was speaking; shouting and weeping. So faint, it could have been his imagination. But it wasn't.

Garth's hands gripped the boulder. Above him, Hinu's eyes were huge and far away.

What was happening? Who was—? Garth shook his head, tried to clear his mind.

43

Hinu had almost reached the boulder. She turned her head down towards him, and he had to look away. He realized she was waiting for him, and clumsily he began to move on. The voices were gone.

They were at the bottom in another fifteen minutes. The gully ended in a two-yard bank, old tree-roots sticking out where the river had sliced soil away. The roots made a rough ladder to the water's edge.

High above them, the smoke stain crept across the sky. Garth shot a look at Hinu while she stooped, tightening her straps to get the pack as high as possible on her shoulders for the river-crossing. Her face was as calm and quiet as always. That wailing and calling: had he imagined it, somehow? Stuff like that just didn't happen! Then he remembered the girl standing at the clearing edge after breakfast – it seemed like another world now – watching the chickadee and that deer. He shivered, and knew it wasn't the cold wind.

They crossed the Pine in threes, arms linked to hold them against the swirling current. Isaac started to loop his arm through Kelsey's, but she pulled away. "Suit yourself," he muttered.

The water was hip-deep and freezing. People yelled words that would have gotten them into trouble at school. They came sloshing out onto the sand on the far side, boots squelching.

"Fire. We gotta start a fire," Max urged. Garth's mind boggled for a moment. Start a fire?? Oh…yeah. Right.

The supervisor had fire starters in his pack. Isaac produced a cigarette lighter from his jacket. (Hmmmm, thought Garth.) The others, teeth chattering, began picking up driftwood from the little bank and the reeds behind. Ten minutes later, they stood in a circle around the blazing wood, jeans and boots steaming.

"Good stuff, people." Max patted Danny and Kelsey on the shoulders. "We'll use this fire for a signal, too. Now we just stay here, we keep our eyes wide open, and we wait for someone to find us."

Above the lip of the cliff, the smoke had spread more thickly. Up there, fire crews with trucks and helicopters would be battling the fire, surrounding it and containing it. The zones they'd driven or run through would be full of men and machines. Down here in the gorge, with river and rocky bluffs to shield them, it was hard to feel involved any more. Clouds still slunk fast across the sky, but the wind hardly touched them as they stood and stared upwards. Garth turned and gazed at the ridges and slopes of pines climbing up behind them. They were safe.

Max had moved over to the edge of the reeds, still trying his cellphone. Garth could tell the supervisor wasn't going to relax till searchers found them and they were safely back at Treecorp headquarters.

Danny took a sandwich from his pack. He hesitated, pulled out another, and passed it to Isaac. The other boy grunted, "Thanks." Danny caught Garth's eye. "I'm starving. I could eat a horse." He glanced at the smoke above. "A roast horse."

Garth gave his friend a bigger grin than the joke deserved. Suddenly, he felt hungry, too. He looked at his watch. 12:20 pm. Half a life had galloped past in the last few hours.

The others also began hauling out lunches and water bottles. He was parched as well, Garth realized. He drained his bottle in eight gulps, water trickling down his filthy chin onto his filthy neck, then took it down to the river to fill. No point in worrying about bugs just now.

Kelsey, the seat of her jeans steaming from the fire, was starting in on Isaac. "Hinu deserves better than you. You and your stupid ATVs!"

It wasn't he who – Garth thought again. But Isaac stood glowering back at Kelsey.

"Yeah? Well, I'm not ending up like my old man. He spends half his life slaving away for Treecorp, like everyone else in this pathetic town. And what happens? He's broken like a twig. Mom can't even look at the forest now."

"So?" the once-blonde girl demanded. "You're a big help, riding around on that stupid machine."

"We made those ATVs. Put them together from old workshop stuff and parts we bought. Me and Je—" Isaac stopped as he began to say a name. He darted a look at Hinu, then at Max, who was picking his way back towards the fire.

"If you're a qualified mechanic, you can go anywhere," Isaac said. "Soon as I can, I'm outta here."

Kelsey sneered. "You'll be lucky if you're outta jail."

Max cut in. "Okay, Kelsey. Enough, huh?"

The girl glared at the supervisor, muttered something, then stalked away.

The smoke above the cliffs had begun to form a ragged line. Everyone fell silent. Garth felt exhaustion pull at him. They stood around the driftwood fire, wet clothes slowly baking dry, and waited for things to be over.

EIGHT

Should he save any food? Garth wondered. How long before search party reached them? And how many people were looking for them? Saving them had to be more important than fighting the fire. He held his last sandwich for a moment, then pushed it and an apple back into his pack.

"You got any lunch left?" he asked Danny. Silly question – his mate nodded with mouth full and held out a cookie. Garth waved it away. "Just wondering."

Max had hardly touched his food. He stood by the glowing driftwood, eyes on the cliff they'd left behind. Guess he doesn't want to miss another chopper, Garth decided. At least it won't have any trouble getting down here; there's thirty yards of reeds and grass between us and the forest, plus plenty of space above the bank to hover. They'd have to put their campfire out first; the downdraft from a chopper's rotors could send burning driftwood flying everywhere.

His jeans were nearly dry now. Kelsey and Danny had

taken off their boots and held steaming socks out towards the heat, but he felt better with his on, somehow. Isaac stood staring into the little fire. What would happen to him? Garth wondered suddenly. Jail or something, like Kelsey said? He and his friend had really messed things up. He'd messed up with Hinu, too.

The dark-haired girl sat on a log, hands out to the warmth. Once again, Garth remembered those voices in the gully. He'd imagined them. Or was it just wind in the trees? No. Something had happened back there. He shivered.

He glanced up once more at the notch in the cliff tops that was the start of the gully, and began to get to his feet. Movement at the edge of the pine zone, shapes appearing out of the trees and darting back again. He opened his mouth to shout, but Danny beat him to it.

"Look! The fire's reached the cliff!"

They were all standing, pulled to their feet by the sight above. A lick of orange coiled up one trunk, and the treetop puffed into flames. A second later, the whooshing sound of a Crown Fire came faintly down to them. Burning needles exploded outwards, faded to black as they whirled into the gulf beyond the cliff. Twenty yards along the line, another treetop flared.

Danny had grabbed his pack. Max stood bent slightly forward, neck turning as his eyes searched the cliff top. Other spots of fire swelled into life among the trunks. Above the pine zone, smoke surged and was torn away like angry surf. Spittings and cracklings reached them. That gully had saved them, all right. They were okay here…right?

"Fill your water bottles." Max began pulling out his own. "Then do up your packs."

Kelsey pushed scorched, scummy hair off her forehead. "What—?"

"Just do it." Max strode down to the river's edge.

The others' faces were blank, though Danny's mouth had started twitching again. Garth felt his guts go cold and heavy once more.

High up on the cliff top, the whole end row of pines were burning. Trees tossed and whipped in the updrafts of heat. Flames danced above the tall crowns, vanishing into purple rolls of smoke. Wind swept the fire aside for a second, so black skeletons of trunks and branches stood against a backdrop of swirling orange that surged back to swallow them. A thrumming and roaring rolled down to the river bank. A rampart of flames reared along the edge of the cliff, beautiful and terrible.

Hinu called out. A long branch fell from its blazing tree, crashing to the ground, scattering glowing shapes ahead of it. Burning pinecones, Garth realized. They plunged down the cliff-face, bouncing from ledges, hissing into the Pine. A couple flew right across the river, to lie smoking on the sand. "Look out!" Garth heard someone gasping. It was him.

"Let's go!" Danny flung his pack on. "Up into the trees!"

Kelsey was snatching up her gear, too. "Yeah, come on!"

"No!" They all stopped at Max's voice. "You don't go uphill to get away from a fire. It can come up ridges faster

49

than you. Plus there are winds that blow up valleys. The fire can burn ahead of you – cut you off."

Kelsey muttered, but put her pack down again. The supervisor watched her for a second, then turned away, staring at the zones of pines behind, where they sloped up towards a row of low crests.

A splintering crack, and they spun round. The whole top of a tree fell in a shower of fire. Burning fragments sailed out across the gulf. They'll go out before they land, won't they? Garth thought. He realized he was hugging himself as he watched. Another big branch crashed, rolled in a fury of sparks across the sloping ground, and dropped down the face of the cliff. Smoke rose on ledges and outcrops where it hit. The rim of the little gully was on fire now. Hinu's hand covered her mouth as she watched. Isaac took a step towards her, then turned away.

Max's voice broke in again. "Get those shovels. Dig trenches in the dirt – deep enough to lie in. We'll get in and cover ourselves with more dirt." He jabbed a finger at the driftwood fire. "Put that out. Come on!"

Hands grabbed for the shovels. Blades crunched into sandy soil. Kelsey's first shovelful flew into Garth's face. He spluttered, swore, bent to his own digging, and stopped.

A sound on the cliff top caused everyone to look up. Two burning trees had begun collapsing at almost the same time. They curved down, one across the other. The top tree shattered, and blazing branches somersaulted down the gully where they'd slithered just an hour before. They hit the boulders, showering cones and bark sideways. Underbrush began to burn.

The largest branch crashed down the narrow passage

end-over-end, like some monstrous burning baton. It hit a ledge and catapulted outwards. A burst of fiery cones and embers filled the air, flying straight at the six observers.

A second of shouts and screams, then everyone was face down on the bank, hugging it, trying to bury heads and bodies in the shallow trenches they'd made. There was dirt in Garth's mouth. Flashes of flame flicked past him. He felt a pulse of heat, heard the splash and angry hiss of cones hitting the river.

Something big crashed onto a rock mid-stream and smacked onto the bank nearby. Their driftwood fire shattered, smoking logs spinning and flaring.

Danny came yelling and flailing to his feet. A burning piece of bark had landed on the back of his sweater. The stink of charred wool reached Garth's nostrils. Just as well it *was* wool. "Drop and roll next time," Max said. "It's the first thing to smother any flames, remember. Drop and roll." The supervisor breathed deeply as he spoke, and Garth realized he was scared, too.

They were all standing now, brushing dirt from clothes, staring at the wreck that had been their fire. All across the bank, the driftwood smoldered and smoked. The half-branch that had landed among them lay still glowing. Hinu rubbed at a scorch mark on her pack.

Fifty yards upstream, another blazing mass plunged down the cliff. From the line of burning, dying trees, the rain of fiery fragments went on, gusting out over the gulf, then floating down. In the reeds behind where they stood, a couple of smoke wisps climbed feebly upwards, then went out. They weren't going to be safe here after all.

NINE

Danny had seized his pack again. "Come *on*! Why are we hanging around here?" Kelsey began stuffing things into her pack once more. "He's right. Let's move, for heaven's sake! I'm not gonna stay and get—"

She stopped, crouched with one arm up over her face as Max strode at her. For half a second, Garth thought the supervisor was going to shake some sense into her. "Don't—" Hinu began. Danny gaped.

Max grabbed the blonde girl's pack, flung it back down on the ground, and stood towering over her. "I said leave it!" he snarled.

Everyone was silent. Even the fire above seemed to get quiet. After a moment, Max turned away, glanced at the smoldering logs strewn over the bank, then looked at the others again. "Okay, we're in trouble. I thought we could stay here, but we can't. The fire's started its own wind-storm up there. Stuff could fall anywhere." He jerked his head at where the Pine churned among its boulders. "We can't get out along the river. There's gorges upstream and downstream – rapids and whirlpools. We—"

They flinched as another tree toppled in a swirl of orange down the cliff, about twenty yards upstream. Smoking fragments curved through the air into river and reeds. Through his shock and the leaden weight in his stomach, Garth knew he would always remember the incredible things he was seeing. Isaac's face was white as he watched. Garth felt a stab of sympathy for the guy. This wasn't really his fault. His useless friend was the one to blame.

Max was talking again, pointing to the forest behind them. "There's a valley on the other side of those hills. A little bit of a river, then a steep ridge that goes up to a cleared patch called Bald Dome. They've got a fire lookout tower there. Might be someone on watch, plus there'll be a phone. We'll head for that."

Hinu and Isaac listened, eyes fixed on the Supervisor. Kelsey rubbed her ruined hair and glared at the world. Danny chewed his bottom lip. On the cliffs, the fire raged on. The air above the river was full of drifting black shards.

"It's gonna be hard." Max checked his watch, and Garth did the same. 1:30 pm. "Take us nearly four hours, so it'll be getting dark by the time we're there. We'll be climbing away from the fire, and you heard me say that's tricky." He pointed to them one by one. "I'm pairing you off as buddies – Hinu and Kelsey; Danny and Garth. You, Isaac or whatever, you're with me," Max rolled his eyes at Isaac and continued. "Everyone keeps an eye on their buddy all the time, okay?"

Danny had already pulled on his pack. Max stared at him for a moment, and held up a hand. "How much food do we have left? Let's total it up."

Hinu had two sandwiches and some cookies. Danny had two sandwiches and a bunch of cookies. Garth had his sandwich and apple. Kelsey had some fruit. Isaac had nothing.

"Give him a couple of cookies, Danny," Max ordered. Isaac started to say, "I don't—" and the Supervisor turned on him. "You take them. I'm not having you petering out when your energy runs low. We're getting you out of here so you can face what you did."

The two of them glared at each other. Max was doing it deliberately, Garth realized. Isaac would keep going on anger. He wondered what would keep the rest of them going.

"Top up those water bottles," Max said. "And drink as much as you can from the river. Drink *more* than you can. You're gonna need it."

They filled their bottles, drank, re-filled them. Isaac crouched at the water's edge, scooping up water like an animal. They all ducked again as more flaming debris bounded down the cliff-face. Evil hisses echoed from upstream. The smell of smoke filled the air. Dirty gray banners of it hid the clouds.

Kelsey watched it as she tightened her water bottle, then shrugged at Garth. "Don't think I'll take up smoking." Garth managed half a grin.

"Make sure your packs sit properly," Max ordered. "Anyone got wet socks? You're going to get blisters. You'll just have to deal with it."

Above him on the cliff top, a big pine flared as its resin exploded. Cones flew like shrapnel, smoke trails arcing down the sky behind them. Some hit the sandy soil on the river bank. Others whizzed overhead and into the reeds. More threads of smoke began to rise from the feathery clumps. This time, they didn't all go out.

How long would it take for the reeds to start burning? How long then till it spread to the zone of pines they were heading into? From now on, it was all about time.

They moved through the reeds in single file. Max led; Garth came last, just behind Danny.

The big bushes sprawled across the sandy earth, making walking tricky. "Watch where you're going," Max told them again. The long, flax-like leaves were damp where they lay close to the ground, but the central plumes looked dry and crackly. Hard to tell how much they would burn.

A chill gust blew through Garth's sweater, and he wrapped his arms around himself again. He'd gotten cold standing on the bank back there.

There was still only a little wind down here at the bottom of the gorge. The less, the better. But up on the cliff at their backs, the blaze sucked oxygen into it, sent flames and sparks whooshing out. If those sparks drifted far into the forest, they could end up with fire ahead of them. Garth tried not to think of—

"Aaah!" Kelsey lurched and grabbed at the reeds, flexing her left ankle. Oh no, clumsy girl! Garth thought. Max was right; if anyone got hurt, they were in big trouble. No, *bigger* trouble.

Danny stood behind her and reached around to hold her elbow as she staggered. Kelsey wrenched away, just as she'd done with Isaac. "I'm fine!"

They moved on, Kelsey limping slightly. Another twenty steps, and the ground began to slope gently upwards. The clumps of sprawling green leaves gave way to scattered pine needles. Ten more yards, and their boots tread a brittle, crunching floor.

At the back of the line, Garth turned for one final look. Already he could see more of the plateau on the far side of the Pine.

It was a place of destruction and ugliness, black and red and orange, glowing and flaring like some terrible nuclear battlefield. The smoke-filled sky over it churned evil and foul. It would be years before this land could be made whole and green again. As he watched, Garth promised himself he would never do anything to harm a single tree, for as long as he lived. Again he tried to imagine how Isaac was feeling.

Ten yards ahead, Danny turned and stared back at him. Hope he doesn't lose it again, Garth thought. Guys aren't supposed to do that sort of thing. The moment the words were in his mind, he felt ashamed, somehow. He hurried after his friend – his buddy – and they passed into the trees.

TEN

In the pines, the world changed once again. Except for the faint stink of burned wool wafting back to him from Danny's sweater, and a distant growling that Garth could hardly hear for the sighing branches overhead, the blaze was just a memory.

But he couldn't believe the feeling of distance and safety any more. The fire could reach anywhere. He remembered one fire that his dad had told him about. It hadraged for a week, across canyons, up and over a mountain range. Fourteen of the firefighters who parachuted in to fight it were killed. Many of them died in a firefighter's nightmare, – a Blow-Up, when several fires met and the air for hundreds of yards around exploded in a furnace of heat. Some had tried to get inside the fire-proof foil shelters they carried, but the heat had been so terrible, the shelters melted. Garth tried not to think of that, either.

They were climbing steadily. Ahead through avenues of trees, the needle-covered ground sloped towards a crest he couldn't see yet. Down the other side of that, Max had said. Across a river and another climb to Bald Dome.

Up front, Max tramped on, turning every few moments

to check the others. He seemed calm now. Isaac loped behind, the sack with its shovel across his back. Then came Kelsey, still limping slightly. Then Hinu and Danny.

The Aboriginal girl's hands were moving. She was touching the pine trunks as she passed. Garth saw her lips fluttering again.

Her ancestors or tribe or whatever had nothing to do with these trees! They were the ones who caused problems when firms like Treecorp tried to develop the forests. All they'd ever had was...was the land.

Garth stared at the great dinosaur-scales of bark as he plodded past the next big pine. He rested his own palm on one of the trunks, felt its thickness and corrugations, touched the old circle of scar where it had been pruned, years ago. Far above, the branches murmured.

He remembered an Aboriginal legend they'd learned about in elementary school – about a Forest God, and how his spirit breathed in every tree. When you touched these trunks, you could feel the power in them. Maybe it was true that...no way, come on!

A chickadee flicked sideways through the air between him and Danny, all plump and cozy and unworried. It was the first bird he'd seen since those fleeing across the firebreak. As long as the chickadees were there, there shouldn't be too much to worry about. If he saw another deer...

Forest gods and deer: he was starting to sound like his mother. This was all such nonsense! He put his head down and trudged on.

It was nearly three o'clock by the time they reached the

crest of the slope. Garth was streaming with sweat under his sweater, and his calf muscles were beginning to ache. Danny seemed OK, but ahead of him, Hinu and Kelsey were struggling.

At one point, as Kelsey hauled herself up a needle-strewn bank, Isaac glanced back, stretched out an arm, yanked her up after him, then began pulling her pack off her shoulders again. Kelsey tried to wrestle away. "Get off!" Max looked around and frowned. "Let him have it. You just walk." Kelsey snarled something at Isaac. Isaac snarled something back at Kelsey. They both toiled on.

When Max called a rest stop, they slumped down on the ground against the rough trunks. "Leave some water," Max called as Danny and Kelsey dragged out their bottles. "There's the river at the bottom, but you'll need a drink on the way down. Eat something." Kelsey began to speak, but the supervisor bulldozed over her. "Shut up! You need to keep your energy up. A cookie or half a sandwich. Just eat!"

As he chewed, Garth stared up past ranks of branches at the sliver of sky. It was a dull sheet of gray now. Smoke or cloud? He couldn't tell. The only smell was the tang of needles and pine resin, and the cool air. The wind had gotten stronger as they climbed higher. The pine tops swung and creaked. Garth tried to imagine what was happening way back behind them. Maybe the fire on the cliff tops would burn itself out. Maybe the river and sandy-soil stretches would be enough to stop it. He pictured those blazing embers sailing through the air, and didn't even want to hope.

The others sat staring at the ground. Isaac's black

helmet lay beside him as he drank from Max's bottle. People had taken off their hard hats and were wiping hands across grimy foreheads. Everyone had sunk into themselves, thinking only of getting to Bald Dome where they might be – they had to be – safe.

Max moved among them, checking. "Ankle okay?" he asked Kelsey, and got a grunt. Garth realized that the soles of his feet felt sore. Those wet socks: he should have dried them, all right.

They started off again after five minutes. Max didn't need to tell them twice. They were exhausted, but they wanted to get away from the fire as fast as possible.

"Downhill for about forty-five minutes now," Max told them. "We'll fill our bottles at the bottom, then it's that last climb. Nobody falls, okay?"

Skidding on needles, grabbing at trunks to brake themselves, they lurched down the slopes. It was easier on the lungs, harder on the feet. After quarter of an hour, Garth knew his right foot was beginning to blister. Ahead, Max called, "Hole!...tree root!" as he went. Kelsey still seemed to be limping but, in their downhill stagger, it was hard to tell. With their eyes on the ground, watching where their feet went, Garth couldn't check the sky. He winced as he felt a blister rip open.

"You okay, man?" Danny was watching him. He'd completely forgotten about keeping an eye on his buddy. Affection for his friend surged through Garth. Danny was scared, but fighting it. They were going to get out of there. "Yeah, I'm fine." He wiped perspiration off his face, flicked it at Danny, and managed a grin. "No sweat, ha!"

On and down they skidded. Weren't they ever going

to reach the bottom? Garth's right foot was raw and throbbing now, and the toes on his left foot hurt as well. What would it be like climbing up the ridge ahead?

"Tree root!...stump!" Garth was starting to hate Max's calls. Why didn't he shut up? He hit angrily at a tree as he slid past. Below him, the others skidded and strode.

Then the light changed, there was an emptiness ahead, and in ten sliding steps they were out in the open. Twenty yards ahead, the next zone of pines angled sharply up towards Bald Dome and help. Right in front of them, a busy channel of water rushed between rocks and clumps of grass. And the scent of smoke hung in the air.

They stood there, sweating, gasping from the downhill rush. Panicky questions tumbled into Garth's mind. Had the fire jumped the Pine? Had it gotten ahead of them? How long did they have? Time, time...

The others could smell the smoke, too. Max stared up and down the little valley. Danny's mouth opened; then he seemed to take a deep breath and hold himself steady. Hinu stood still. Since they'd left the gorge, she hadn't spoken a word aloud.

Garth found himself staring along the mossy boulders of the little river as if at any moment, fire might start snaking and wreathing there. He jumped as Max spoke.

"Don't worry, guys. Valleys like this are wind channels; they'll carry a scent for miles ahead of anywhere else. You get a bit of a breeze coming up here, and you can smell the burgers and fries from Kinross. Valleys and ridges stuff up wind flow in a major way. Let's just stay focused, huh?"

Suddenly, Garth felt better. He stared up at the gray

mat of cloud dragging itself across the sky. Not a sign of smoke. Max was right. They simply had to keep thinking about getting up the next hill to Bald Dome. Things didn't have to get worse.

"Fill those bottles again, okay?" The supervisor's words got them all moving. Danny stooped beside a bunch of ferns and began dipping his bottle into an eddy of freezing water. Beside him, Isaac slurped from cupped hands. He and Hinu hadn't looked at each other for the last half hour. Man, thought Garth, if *I* were going out with her, I'd make sure...

He paused, mouth half-open as he heard the words inside his head. They vanished as Kelsey began shoving past him, climbing on to a rock in the middle of the stream. That's right, water was always supposed to be more bug-free there than at the edges. Oh well, Garth had already decided he couldn't be bothered about bugs just now.

He straightened up. His back was getting chilled already. The moment they stopped moving, the coolness of the day crept in. 3:50 pm; the sun had dropped below the hill behind them. At the very top of the ridge they still had to climb, tree-tops glowed gold.

Come on, Garth urged silently. Let's move. Let's get there.

Then just a couple of yards upstream, Hinu did speak.

"Kels—" There was a slithering sound, a thump, a half-yell. Kelsey lay sprawled between two mossy rocks. Her left ankle, the one she'd hurt crossing the reeds, was twisted underneath her. Her face was stiff with pain.

I was wrong, Garth told himself. Things are going to get a whole lot worse.

ELEVEN

Hinu crouched, helping Kelsey up. The girl tried to stand as if nothing had happened, then hissed as she put weight on her left leg. Danny and Garth sloshed out into the water, took an elbow each, supported her as she hobbled back to the bank. This time, Kelsey didn't try to pull away. Her lips were squeezed together; her mouth was white at the corners.

The stream water was icy inside Garth's boots. Jeez, he told himself, I just got these socks dry! His blistered feet stung and throbbed. Wind blew cold through his sweater, and sudden despair gripped him. He felt more fragile and miserable than he had ever had in his life.

Max's fingers probed Kelsey's ankle as she sat on the ground. Garth pulled the first aid kit from his pack, and passed it to the supervisor. Max nodded. "Thank you." He began strapping tape around the girl's foot and boot. "Get some cold water," he told Isaac. "Pour it on he foot." Cold water, Garth thought. Her whole foot will turn to ice and drop off.

Kelsey struggled to stand again. "I'll be—" She cried out suddenly, a noise of sheer pain that held everyone still for a second. Then Isaac was beside her, pouring water from his motorcydle helmet over her ankle. She gasped. "Typical guys," she managed to say. "Bunch of wet drips." She gasped again, and pressed her lips together harder.

Max turned to the others. "Danny, Garth – find a branch she can use for walking. You, Isaac, carry her pack."

"Leave me here," protested Kelsey. "The chopper can pick me up when you radio. You guys keep—"

The supervisor ignored her. "We'll take turns to help. Ten minutes each." He jerked his head at the injured girl. "You concentrate on moving. Shut everything else out of your mind. We're gonna get to Bald Peak and that clearing. And that phone."

Just five minutes after they started climbing again, Garth understood it was going to be harder than anything he'd ever known. He was the first to help Kelsey as she struggled up into the pines. Danny carried his pack. Garth clamped his left arm round the girl's waist, trying to take as much of her weight as he could. He felt the warmth of her hip and side. Her cheek brushed his. The smell of her charred hair filled his nostrils. He remembered that burn on the back of his own hand; it was just a distant sting now.

Kelsey gripped the fallen pine branch that Danny had found by the stream edge, stabbing it into the thin, needle-strewn soil with each step. She'd closed her eyes. Half-stopped cries burst from her each time her left foot touched the ground. In the cold air, her forehead was wet with perspiration. Behind her, Hinu kept her hands on Kelsey's hips and bottom, helping push her up, steadying her when she lurched. No way am I doing that, Garth decided. I'll get my head smacked off!

They were all sweating and panting. Garth's feet burned. He couldn't tell if the wetness in his boots was perspiration or water. Or blood. This slope was steeper than the last ridge. Their feet skidded on needles. A few times, they had to haul themselves up by the tree-roots that clutched claw-like at the ground.

They stopped after half an hour. Danny, who'd been taking his turn helping Kelsey, leaned against a tree-trunk, dragging in air. The girl slumped on the ground, head between knees.

"Drink," Max told them as he shrugged off Danny's pack. I can't, Garth knew. I'll just spit it up again. "Drink!" the supervisor ordered again. Garth pulled out his water bottle, hands shuddering as he undid it. He swallowed, then passed it again to Isaac. The stubbly head nodded.

Smoke, Garth realized suddenly. I can smell smoke again. Or could he? Maybe it was from Kelsey's burned hair. Maybe it was from people's dirty, smelly clothing. Then, as he lifted his head and leaned it against a trunk, breath still laboring in his chest, he saw that Max was standing, face turning one way, then the other, breathing carefully through his nose. Their eyes met, and some sort of understanding passed between them.

"Okay." The others groaned as Max spoke. "On your feet. Move on."

This time Isaac led, the sack with its shovel across his back,

Kelsey's pack and her yellow hard hat swinging beside it. He carried Hinu's pack and helmet in one hand as well. "Keep following the ridge," Max ordered him. "You got us into this; you're going to help get us out." The bony boy just turned and started walking.

As he watched Isaac start off, Garth thought of the words that had rushed into his mind just before Kelsey fell. But he hadn't got time for stuff like that now. He moved to help the injured girl, as she winced to her feet with Hinu gripping her elbows, then stopped as Max silently mouthed, "No." The supervisor spoke to Danny. "You and Hinu help her for another five minutes. Then we'll give you a decent rest." Garth's friend just nodded, too. There was no sign of panic from him now. No sign of anything. He seemed to have pulled back, deep inside himself.

As the others started trudging upwards again, Max dropped back a few yards, Garth beside him. The supervisor's face was pinched and watchful. His eyes checked all directions. He's still twitchy, Garth knew. It made his own guts clench again.

"All right," the supervisor kept his voice low; the treetops sighed and groaned above them. "You and your dad know about forests. I hadn't expected to smell smoke back there. You probably hadn't, either."

Garth said nothing. Max glanced back down through the pines. "It could be miles away. But we gotta face the fact – it might have gotten across the Pine."

Something cold touched Garth's back. He listened, trying to take in what Max was saying.

"Like I said, fire travels faster uphill. So that slope we've just come down should slow it. But in the valley, anything could happen."

He paused, lifting his head to listen, breathing slowly through his nose again. Garth couldn't be sure. Was there smoke? Or...But Max was murmuring to him once more.

"Keep your eyes and ears open. If you notice anything, tell me. Not the others. If we have to, we'll dig in where we are, try to shelter, then break out onto the burned ground. I'm hoping it won't come to that, though. Fingers crossed, eh?"

He gave Garth a nod, then strode forward after the others, where they panted and labored ahead. "Okay, Danny, I'll give you a rest. Come on, Kelsey – fit young thing like you, you should be skipping up here!"

At the rear, Garth plodded on. He was limping too, now. His feet ached each time they touched the ground.

His mind tried to understand what Max had just said. He knew what the supervisor meant about burned ground. If anyone was totally trapped by a forest fire, they could try sprinting through the flames into the smoking blackness where the blaze had already been. It was desperation stuff only. He tried to imagine Kelsey doing it, and couldn't.

He was supposed to be keeping eyes and ears open. He swung around, face twisting as his right foot caught and tore inside the boot. Nothing to see but the ridge dropping away behind them. Nothing to hear but the branches knocking and shushing above. Smoke? He couldn't be sure.

Ahead of him, the others kept battling upwards, heads

down, feet slipping, breath rasping. Garth pushed after them. The world had dwindled to this: the thin slope beneath his raw feet; the struggle and slip of his damp, stained boots. Hawaii and the school trip were somewhere on the other side of the Universe now. Kinross and home, too.

Treecorp would have reported them missing hours ago. His mom and dad would know something was terribly wrong. Suddenly, Garth's whole body longed to be safely home. He wished his parents were there to hold him. Other half thoughts jumbled in his mind. Had Leah's gang gotten out? Was the fire maybe under control already? Fires really stank when they were put out; maybe that was why they'd smelt smoke back there?

His head jerked round as something boomed behind him. The fire – no, the wind, blowing stronger again as they climbed higher, sending treetops swinging and colliding.

"Take two." Max spoke from up ahead, easing Kelsey down against a tree. The girl's eyes were glazed, her face slack with pain. Hinu knelt beside her with a water bottle, murmuring as Kelsey tried to turn her head away, pouring a little into her friend's mouth. Danny slid down against another pine. At the front, Isaac sat, head bent.

We can't go on much longer, Garth knew. Even if the fire is still going and starts up the slope after us, we can't keep going like this.

But they did. On and up, slipping and panting. Garth noticed how much darker it was among the tall pines. At least in the late afternoon, when the temperature dropped, the fire would burn more slowly. Time still mattered.

Ahead of him, Danny halted and leaned against a trunk, eyes closed, breath sobbing. Garth took his elbow. "Come on, man." Danny stayed slumped. He shook his head feebly.

Garth's own fear rose suddenly inside him. "Come on!" He hauled Danny away from the tree, shoved him on up the slope. The other boy lurched, then plodded on, head down. Garth followed, staring at the ground too.

When he pushed back his sleeve another thirty steps later, and made his eyes focus on his watch, the figures read 4:48 pm. Sun would be setting soon: not that he could see any sun in the grayness glimpsed through tossing treetops. They couldn't have far to go now, surely. They couldn't.

It was taking all his strength to keep his raw feet moving. He kept forgetting to check behind them. When he remembered, he turned and stared with blurry eyes into ranks of dark-green and gray columns, angling back down to the stream.

Ahead, Danny was stumbling, grabbing at roots and trunks, but kept going. Hinu labored on. Sometimes Garth saw her mouth forming silent words. He didn't care what they were any longer.

Max was almost carrying Kelsey now, though she still tried to push with the pine branch at the slope. Isaac, jeans ripped and filthy, stupid helmet stuffed into the sack on his back now, climbed ahead, dropped packs, slid back to help Max pull and push Kelsey up a clay bank. He's in good shape, Garth's mind managed to think. Weird, really – if this fire business hadn't started, Isaac would be quite a cool guy to be in the forest with.

The ground grew steeper still. On hands and knees, Garth hauled himself up. Kelsey was sobbing. The others struggled, slipped, clambered on.

Someone called out to him. Hinu. No, not her. It was… And then the voices he'd half heard in the little gully were all around him again. This time there was no doubt. There were dozens of them, men and women and children, terrified and defiant. They wailed and lamented and sang encouragement to one another. The steep slope rang with them.

Garth clutched the trunk of a tree. There was nothing he could see, but he knew now. These were Hinu's people. What she'd said was true. They—

"Come on, Garth!" Max stood panting and glaring back at him. Isaac and Danny had turned to stare too. Garth tried to say something, failed, and staggered on up the slope.

After five minutes, he took another look back. The smell of smoke was no stronger. Away to one side, a band of red flashed as the sun began to sink behind a ridge. Garth turned his aching neck and staggered upwards again.

People had started talking ahead. Isaac, then Max. Oh no, what was wrong now? Max was supposed to be such an expert; couldn't he even get them to where they were heading? Garth bent, head down, panting and heaving, then forced himself to look up the ridge.

A tree rose in front of him. A weird, skeleton-like tree, half visible through the rows of pines, taller and grayer than the others. Not a tree. The steel struts of a fire-watching tower.

Another dozen stumbling steps, and they were out

70

in the open, the slope leveling out. Bald Dome stretched around them, a scraped clay hilltop the size of a soccer field, dotted with grassy tufts and a few shrubs. The fire tower stood near one side of the clearing, a squat, shed-sized wooden cabin beside it.

Garth stood trembling, trying to understand that they'd made it. Around him, the other five panted and stared. A cool gust blew, and suddenly they were all shivering. Garth turned for one final check of the ridge they'd toiled up, and stood very still.

The trees on the ridge bent in the wind, shadowy and tall. Far back behind them, the horizon was on fire.

TWELVE

It hasn't stopped, Garth kept saying to himself as he stared. It isn't out. It isn't over.

Two – three? – ridges away, an orange line flickered and pulsed above the pines. Rows of treetops, made tiny by distance, stood against the glow. Black streamers that must be smoke swirled upwards into the darkening sky and disappeared.

Off to one side, on a plateau further away, more zones of pines blazed. The sky above them quivered, reflecting red and purple onto the inferno below. Further across, behind a different ridge, another orange arc grew in the sky. Flames were swarming up the far side.

The fire was across the Pine River, Garth realized. And it had divided and grown; the emergency crews would be fighting at least three or four blazes now, blazes that raced in different directions as the slope of the land and the windstorms created by the fires pulled them along. If they turned and came together…a Blow-Up! It must not happen. The others stood staring at the distant fires. Staring and swaying. Garth felt their fear, felt fear pull at him as well.

"Come on." Max moved towards the cabin. Garth's blisters caught and ripped again as he followed. Danny stumbled beside him; they didn't look at each other.

The wooden shed was empty; Garth knew that by the blank windows and the shut door. Above it, the steel struts of the tower rose towards an enclosed metal platform ten yards up.

Max banged on the cabin door, waited, banged again. No reply. He lifted one foot, lined it up the lock, drew it back, and kicked it. The lock wrenched and snapped; the door sagged open. "They can take it out of my wages," the supervisor grunted. He jerked a thumb at the dark little interior. "Be my guests."

They crowded inside, Kelsey biting her lip as she leaned on her branch. One narrow bunk; a table with a candle; two chairs; a bottled gas stove; a cupboard. Above the cupboard, held to the wall by clips and labeled TREECORP PROPERTY: EMERGENCY USE ONLY – a cellphone.

"See if there's anything to eat," Max said as he pulled the phone down and began pressing buttons. Almost immediately he began speaking. "Who's this? Pio? Pio, it's Max. We're at Bald Dome. Me and the kids. We're okay." Garth saw relief softening the others' faces.

There were two packets of peanuts in the cupboard. A bag with a few carrots, and a tube of condensed milk. They all began sucking and chewing. Garth still felt sick with exhaustion, but almost immediately, energy started seeping back. So did hope. They weren't alone any longer; somebody knew about them.

Danny began mumbling to him. "Sorry I—" Garth

shook his head. "Doesn't matter. It's okay" He realized Hinu was watching from across the room. She gave a half-nod. Did she somehow know he'd heard those voices? Bits of what Max was saying came to his ears. "Leah... ankle injury...fire-front...chopper."

Kelsey half-sprawled on the bunk, Hinu beside her. Danny had dropped down on one of the chairs as if he'd never get up again. Isaac sat on the floor by the leaning, broken door. He'd been part of them as they fought their way up the hill; now he was separate again. Garth tried to think of something to say to him, but his mind was mush. Man, he thought yet again. Am I gonna have some stories to tell! He realized Max was talking to them, and tried to listen.

"The good news first, people. Leah's gang are out safe. And there's a chopper coming to get us."

Again, Garth saw the others' faces change, the smiles started. They stopped as Max held up a hand.

"Now the not-so-good news. It won't be till daylight. The fire's almost across the main road in some places. If it gets into the forest on the other side, it'll probably reach Kinross. They've got to stop that from happening. All the choppers are using huge buckets on it. Soon as they possibly can, they'll send the one with night-landing capability for us."

He paused, rubbed a bristly, grimy jaw. "The weather forecast is still talking about rain, but it isn't here yet. They're keeping an eye on the wind."

Max looked around. Hinu had lit the candle with matches from the window sill. A circle of scratched cheeks and sunken eyes gazed back at him. "We'll be okay here till morning. If the fire gets close enough to be a worry, we'll dig ourselves in, in the clearing." He shook his head as Danny started to speak. "We can't stay in a wooden cabin, my friend."

Silence. Then heads turned as Isaac spoke. "I'm sorry. Look, I know it's not a lot of good right now, but I'm really sorry."

Kelsey gave a snort. The others stared at the candle flame, except for Hinu, who watched Isaac. After a moment, Max went, "Ah well..." He stretched. "You all check the water and food. We'll need to take turns watching the direction the fire's moving. I'll leave the cellphone here. I'm gonna check out our situation more closely."

Hinu held up a packet. "Found some lasagna in the cupboard."

Garth sighed to himself. He hated lasagna. Lasagna made him want to throw up. Except...except tonight he couldn't wait to eat lasagna.

Max took a shovel and headed outside into the now-dark evening, propping the broken door half-closed behind him. Isaac and Hinu bent over the bottled-gas stove, doing things with the lasagna. Garth looked at their two heads close together, then looked away, to where Kelsey and Danny still sprawled on bunk and chair. He sat, eased off his boots and began working his socks down over his feet, biting his lip as they snagged on raw flesh.

When the first one was off, he swallowed. The sole of his foot was a blotch of blisters, red and weeping or white and swollen. Blood caked the inside of his sock. When he'd peeled off the other, the foot inside it looked almost as bad.

"Gross!" Kelsey was watching him. "Mr. Gross Feet! And I thought I looked disgusting!"

"My feet, your hair," Garth said. "Good match." He tried to grin, but his mouth felt shaky. Kelsey didn't look any better. Thank God that chopper was coming. In his head, he began trying to count the hours till first light.

"The fire will burn slower at night." It wasn't till he saw the others staring, that Garth understood he'd spoken aloud. He felt a total geek, then made himself continue remembering what his father had told him once. "It's true – the cool air sinks down like a blanket over the flames. They can't burn as high or as fast."

Nobody spoke for a moment. Then Hinu, eyes on the saucepan she was slowly stirring, said, "When my great-great-grandfather and the others escaped across the river, they climbed up the hills through the bush till they came to a high, clear place." She gazed out at the darkness beyond the window, and the thin, evil flicker along the skyline. "I wonder if it was here? They hid for days, till they had no food or water left. Then their gods sent rain so they could drink. And then…" She gazed through the window again.

As he stared at the girl, and the blackness into which she was looking, Garth remembered those voices in the little gully and on the hillside. He'd never forget them.

Hinu glanced at him suddenly. Had she—? Garth jumped as the cellphone rang.

"Who's this?" a man's voice asked. "Garth – you're Monty's kid? We've told your mom and dad you're okay. This is just to confirm that the chopper's coming at first light. Max there?"

"He's outside checking things," Garth replied. The others were watching him; he felt a sudden swell of importance.

"Get him to call in, will you, Garth? There's five of you, right?"

"Six," Garth said. "Max, me, Hinu, Danny, Kelsey. And Isaac."

A second's silence at the other end. Garth heard paper turning. "Who's Isaac?"

Now Garth felt awkward, not important. "He...he was on one of the ATVs."

"Right," said the voice after a pause. "Well, you tell Isaac we're really looking forward to meeting him when he gets back here."

Max came back into the hut ten minutes later, bringing a wave of cool night air with him. The lasagna had vanished in thirty seconds, except for a tiny helping kept for him. Garth knew now that lasagna was the best food in the galaxy.

"I've started" to clear some ground in the middle of the bare patch," the supervisor said. "There's pines all round the clearing, except for one zone where they were felled about six or seven years back, but they're a good distance away. If we need to, we just dig ourselves a decent hole and we'll be fine."

Garth watched, trying to make out the big man's expression, but the candle light filled his face with shadows.

"We need to keep watching those fire-fronts," Max went on. "Two people. An hour at a time. Take an extra jacket with you."

"I'll go," Garth said.

"Me too." Danny struggled up from the chair, then reeled and almost fell. The boy's face was green and pale with exhaustion. Max grabbed his elbow and sat him down again. "Not just yet, Danny."

Isaac fished a tiny shred of lasagna from the pot. "I'll go."

Kelsey's snort sounded a fraction stronger. "Bit late to be hoping for brownie points."

Before he knew he was saying it, Garth heard his own voice. "Thanks, Isaac."

The boy didn't look at either of them. He pulled on the parka that Danny held out. "Take a couple of shovels, eh?" Max said. "You can keep warm getting rid of the growth in the clearing. I've already started it."

It was hard to leave the snug warmth of the cabin and step outside into the cold darkness. The skeleton of the fire-watch tower climbed into a black sky above them. A break in the pines on the far side of the clearing must be the felled area that Max had mentioned. Along the skyline and behind ridges in the distance, the orange-red glows trembled and crept. Garth couldn't tell if they'd moved any closer. Maybe the winds were pushing them away. He was almost too exhausted to care.

Isaac was watching the far-off flames, too. "They'll lock me up and throw away the key," he muttered. Garth didn't know what to say.

They moved across the bare ground, Garth limping on his raw feet, looking for where Max had begun clearing. If the fires did come swarming up Bald Dome, they needed as big an area as possible where they could huddle in the ground: an area with no fuel around for heat to reach them. The dim square of candle-lit window shrank behind them. Finally Garth made out a scraped patch ahead, fringed with chopped-out clumps of grass and tall weeds. "Here it is."

They set to work, hacking down and digging up more of the shin-high growth, chucking it towards the edges of the clearing. As their eyes grew used to the blackness, they were able to work faster, warming up in spite of the wind slicing past.

"Ah, well." Isaac spoke again. "I'll definitely have to get away from Kinross after this, right?"

Garth understood that the other boy was talking mainly to himself. But almost before he knew he was doing so, he asked, "Is your dad dead?"

He felt Isaac shrug. "Might as well be. He needs a cane to walk. He just sits at home and drinks most of the time." A pause. "Treecorp were pretty good, but after a while, people stopped coming round. Can't blame them; they've got other things in their lives."

Garth stood, shovel in hand, watching the fire lick along the horizon. For a second, it glowed brighter in one place, then dimmed again. A tree must have erupted. It was so weird, watching what was happening, listening to this guy talk.

"What are *you* gonna do?" Isaac's question startled Garth. "You gonna spend the rest of your life in Kinross?"

"Dunno." He'd never thought about it. The timber town was where he'd lived all his life. He supposed...Garth stopped. Something pale had moved among the pines behind the cabin. He kept watching, but nothing else happened. Must have been a branch. The wind blew again;

it was veering all over the place. Garth bent down, chopped at a clump of grass. Doing this was so weird, too.

Isaac started talking again. Garth wondered how long he'd been bottling everything up. "My friend Jeb..." He went silent as the name slipped out, then carried on. "We'd planned to get a place in the city when we had a bit of money. Start up our own ATV-building business. Maybe Hinu..." He stopped again. "Anyway, that's why I use mom's name – get away from everything to do with this hick town. Big deal; it's all over now."

With his shovel, he flung more weeds and grass towards the trees. Garth tried to think of something to say; tried to imagine what was going to happen to Isaac and his friend. But his brain was too tired to work properly.

Far behind them, too distant to hear, the fire-fronts crawled. Time was still the most important thing, Garth realized. Time would wear away the long night. Time would bring first light, and the chopper.

THIRTEEN

They scraped and hacked for another forty-five minutes, maybe, chucking weeds and grass clumps outwards in an ever widening circle, stooping in the darkness to see if that was a grass clump or a lump of clay. A bare area as big as a house now surrounded them.

Boots crunched through the brush, and Max's tall shape approached, turning up the collar of his jacket against the wind that still switched from one direction to another. Garth glanced upwards. No stars. No way of knowing if the clouds hiding them were rain clouds.

"Good stuff," the supervisor told them – both of them. "Okay, go and get some sleep. A couple of the others can take next turn."

All three stood for a moment, watching the far-off pulses of orange and their reflections on the sky. From this distance, they looked almost peaceful. But Garth remembered branches flaming down into the Pine, and the cones like burning tracer bullets. He knew what was happening inside that glow. All those fire crews and choppers fighting it: they would win.

He and Isaac picked their way back towards the cabin, past the high steel struts of the tower. Garth stumbled on a clump of clay, and his right foot throbbed.

Inside the cabin, Hinu sat drowsing on one of the chairs. Garth saw the curve of cheek, the long dark eyelashes. She's cute, he thought. How come I never noticed that before? Isaac was watching the girl, too.

Suddenly, Garth couldn't decide which he wanted most – that Isaac had never been mixed up in starting the fire, or that he and Hinu had never met. Jeez, what was he thinking?

Hinu half-woke as their boots clattered; gazed at them without really seeing them; closed her eyes again. Kelsey and Danny lay huddled on bunk and floor. Kelsey turned over in her sleep; moaned as her left leg bent; slept on.

Isaac passed him a peanut. As Garth bit into it, he checked his watch. 8:45 pm. It felt more like midnight. The other boy was already folding himself down on the floor. The sack in which he'd carried the shovel was under his head. Garth lay down too, wedging himself between Danny and the chair where Hinu dozed. He didn't take his boots off; he wasn't sure he could get them on again. I won't sleep, he knew. It's too cold and uncomfortable, and I'm too tensed up. I won't sleep.

His mother passed him a plate heaped with fried potatoes and corn fritters. Sweet – his favorites! The tablecloth was clean; his clothes were clean; his hands were clean. Radio Forestland played in the kitchen.

At the other end of the table, his father read the paper. "They're well ahead with replanting the burned areas.

They're spraying new trees straight into the ground from helicopters."

Spraying new trees into the ground, Garth thought. Weird! The phone rang, and he reached for it. It rang again, his hand touched the bare boards of the hut floor, and his parents and home vanished.

His watch read 10:20 pm. Hinu was murmuring into the cellphone. "He's outside. I'll get him." Garth saw her picking her way over the huddled bodies towards the broken door. Take the phone with you, he tried to say, but he was sliding down into sleep again.

A bit later, Max was in the cabin and talking on the phone. "How far... time." That's right, Garth remembered. Time was important, because...because...

Movement woke him next. Kelsey was trying to get up, but Max had stopped her. "You stay there." Danny stood by the table, yawning till his face seemed about to turn inside-out. He and Hinu took a shovel each, and moved off into the darkness.

For a moment, Garth felt jealous. Then he felt puzzled. They were coming back in again, banging the door. No, it was wind. 11:27 pm. Seven hours till first light. Maybe six-and-a...he couldn't count; the figures kept fading.

The chopper was here. Garth heard its rotors thudding outside the cabin. He smelt its exhaust. The crew called to him.

So suddenly that he heard himself cry out, he jolted awake, pulling himself half-up, colliding with Isaac, who was struggling up beside him. His legs and arms shook; his back crawled. It was smoke that he smelt. And the

83

noise wasn't a chopper. It was wind, thumping at the cabin walls.

Danny stopped shaking him and squatted opposite. His face was set; his eyes sunk. Garth stared again at his watch. 1:42 in the morning! He'd slept and slept.

Max had just pushed the cellphone back into its clips. Everyone was awake: Kelsey swung her legs over the edge of the bunk. She sat flexing her ankle and wincing.

"We have a change of situation, people." Deep lines crossed Max's face. He hadn't slept at all, Garth realized. How much longer could the supervisor keep going?

"The wind's switched right around and gotten stronger." The supervisor jerked his head at the cabin wall as another gust whacked it. "Should be rain with it, but that hasn't arrived yet."

He looked at them for a second. "It's moving the fire towards us. They've almost contained things along the main road, but there's a problem with the night capability chopper – ash in the rotor mechanism. This wind means the others can't get to us in the dark. They still plan to get one in here at first light, but we gotta take precautions. We gotta dig."

Silence. Garth half-knew what he meant, but his mind didn't want to take it in. He forced himself to listen as Max spoke again.

"We'll dig six slit trenches in that part we've cleared. Just long enough and wide enough for you to fit in. As deep as you can make them. If you need to, you get in, scrape the dirt back over you, cover your head with a sweater or shovel blade. Anything to hold off the radiant heat. It's that heat we gotta stop."

Another wind-thump against the hut. Inside it, nobody spoke. Max gave them a moment, then went on. "So it's one trench each. The smaller the area, the less chance of fire swirling into it. You lie face down. Cooler air stays in the bottom. Bury your face in the dirt if you need to."

He watched them in turn, then took a deep breath. "We shouldn't have to use them. We're just taking precautions, remember. That chopper will be here as soon as it can. Okay, bring everything with you. Hard hats and shovels."

Once more it was hard to leave the cabin. "Anybody got any metal jewelry?" Max asked as they bunched at the door. "Necklaces? Rings? Take them off if you have."

Garth swallowed. He knew why. Radiant heat – hot metal – burns. He didn't want to imagine flames getting that close. He glanced at his watch on its leather strap, then pushed his sweater down over it.

The moment they stepped outside, the cool air blew through their clothing. The wind whipped them. Above their heads, it whined through the metal web of the tower.

The smell of smoke was much stronger. And when Garth turned to look at the horizon, he felt his whole body lock rigid. Everything had changed.

The ridgeline, behind which orange light had glowed before, was now a flickering crest of flame, creeping and dripping like lava. It was the first one they had climbed from Pine River this – no, yesterday afternoon, Garth realized. The near side of the forest was burning. A bloom of flame rose suddenly on the ridge top as he stared. Another resin-packed pine had exploded.

85

Far off to one side, the plateau was still a sweep of fire. In the other direction, a second ridge burned. That fire also was closer.

For the first time since they crouched on the little bank beside the Pine, he could hear the blaze: a thin hiss and crackle, like snakes coiling. Then the wind dropped for a moment, and he heard its other sound – the distant rumble of thousands of trees burning.

They were moving towards the cleared area, Garth hobbling on his blistered feet, Kelsey supporting herself with a shovel. Danny and Hinu looked half asleep. Into Garth's mind came the memory of fleeing people, of voices all around him. God's sending rain, he thought. I wish.

In the darkness, they started to dig.

Garth knew he was getting blisters on his hands as well. The clay was heavy and hard. They had to use their shovels like axes, chopping it into chunks before scooping it out.

Around him, he could hear the others panting, their shovels scraping and clanking. Max stooped over his trench, or came to check how the others were getting on. Around the clearing, pines bent and swung. Wind whined through the tower.

When Max called, "Take five, everyone. Drink time." Garth's trench was maybe thigh-deep. Isaac's and Danny's were about the same; Hinu's half as much. Kelsey's was hardly a scrape; the blonde girl had to set herself before each swing of the shovel. Garth heard her gasp each time its impact jarred her.

He gulped water, stared at his watch. 3:57 am!! They'd been digging for two hours. Only another three hours until first light.

Max was on the cellphone; he'd been muttering into it every twenty minutes or so. Garth straightened his aching back and stared at the crawling fire fronts. The one on the plateau – was it fainter? Yes, it was; they'd dowsed the flames, or maybe lit a burn-back fire to use up fuel before the main blaze could reach it. Then Garth turned his eyes towards the other fires, and a chill touched his back again. The one on yesterday's ridge had moved nearly halfway down the slope. Trees would be toppling there; flaming cones carrying the fire down the slope ahead of the main blaze. The moment it got across the stream, it would come charging up the ridge towards Bald Dome. Two minutes after four. The chopper *had* to come. Even if the night-visibility one wasn't working, couldn't they fit searchlights on another chopper or something?

The others were digging again. Max hacked at Hinu's trench while she scooped out the clay. Garth began chopping into his. Six minutes after four.

By 4:31 am, his trench was hip-deep. He had to stop while he sucked in air. He wiped sweat and dirt from his face, and stared into the pines and the strip of felled trees. Whatever he'd seen earlier – *if* he had seen anything – it wasn't there any more.

4:48 am. Something caught in his throat, and he coughed. Smoke. He dug harder. The wind thwacked past.

5:04 am. His trench was waist-deep. He called to Max, who glanced over and nodded. Garth moved across to Kelsey's, where Isaac was already chopping at the clay while she tried to lift out the dirt. The girl's mouth hung open; in the darkness, her eyes seemed half-closed.

Isaac bent and chopped, dug and flung. He's an okay guy, Garth thought once more. If only...

5:48 am. Kelsey's trench had reached almost hip-deep. Danny was working on it too, now. Then all digging suddenly stopped. Everyone turned, facing the ridge they'd struggled up yesterday afternoon. Down below, the resin of a pine tree was roaring. The fire had swarmed down the opposite slope, and crossed the little river where Kelsey fell.

"Scrape some loose dirt beside the trench!" Max called. "You can use it to cover yourself with."

Their shovels scooped and raked at the ground beside the narrow slits. Every muscle in Garth's body ached now. His hands hurt so much, he had to force them to grip the handle.

He straightened up once more, dared to look around, and the shock of what he saw gripped him tight. Another fire had begun. Over to one side, well away from the ridge, a faint red stain was creeping up the sky. They were going to be surrounded.

He looked again. This light was different. It didn't flicker and move like the other fire-fronts: it was a steady red line.

He lifted his arm, pulled the sweater sleeve back from his watch, and understood. 6:17 am. The first hint of sunrise. Day on one side; the fires on the other. It was still all about time.

FOURTEEN

Darkness still covered the rest of the sky, but the shapes of the pines could be made out now. Dawn was near. Max began talking into the cellphone again. His voice sounded even more urgent. A sweep of wind drowned his words, and suddenly they were all coughing.

Now Garth could see the smoke. In the thinning darkness, it poured up from the valley, coils of sooty brown against the last of the night sky, dimming the swaying treetops, drifting into the clearing. Max turned his back on it; hunched over the phone.

Garth pictured the fire down in the valley, marching up the slope faster than a person could run, pushed by its own updraft. There was nothing to stop it before the clearing: no downward slopes, no water. From somewhere, he remembered his father's story about the campers who didn't pour their boiling coffee water over a grass fire because they thought that only cold water would put it out. He half-giggled stupidly, but choked it back as Hinu glanced at him.

Max thrust the phone into his jacket pocket and called to them. "Chopper's on its way! Be here in twenty minutes, maximum."

Twenty minutes. Garth knew they would be the longest minutes of his life.

Even above the wind, they could hear the fire climbing towards them now. The air shook as if a giant train was rumbling through a tunnel. Max began shouting instructions about the helicopter. "It probably won't land – can't see the ground properly. They'll lower a sling – might be a pick-up guy on it. Kelsey, you go first. Then Hinu. I'll signal—"

They all turned aside, coughing as more smoke swept into the clearing. It bulged out from between the trees, rolled past them in fat cushions of darkness, turning the slowly-paling sky gloomy again. It streamed on, and the light grew once more. Dawn was spreading minute by minute. The red band along the horizon was wider.

So was the other red glow. They could feel it coming. A bright speckle filled the air above the pines, then faded. Burning needles, tossed on the wind. A Crown Fire could start other blazes twenty yards ahead of its own front with such needles, the two sets of flames charging towards each other to meet in a raging updraft.

"The chopper might come in over to one side of the clearing!" Max yelled. "The front of the fire moves faster than its flanks, so the pilot will have to watch for that. Make sure your hard hat's on, in case the chopper drags you into the trees."

Seven minutes gone. Garth glanced at the trenches

they'd sweated over for hours. Jeez, he hoped they didn't have to—

Something dark flashed past. More needles? No: birds. Like yesterday, flicking across the clearing and into the pines on the far side, away from the fire. Garth watched them vanish.

Then he saw it. Among the trees where the birds had flown, a paleness moved. It paused, moved again. A deer stepped out into the clearing, head moving from side to side. It stared at the six humans for a moment. It looked towards the pines from which the smoke was pouring, turned and trotted away into the felled area, jumping easily over stumps and mounds.

Had anybody else seen it? No, they were all focused on the trees. Except for Hinu – she stood watching the animal disappear. Garth thought of that other deer yesterday. Was it…He didn't know what he wanted to ask.

He swung around as voices shouted. Even as he moved, he knew they weren't human. A rumbling and roaring filled his ears. He flung up an arm as brightness filled the sky. The fire was above the trees.

A second ago, there had been only smoke. Now a whirlwind of flame surged over the pine tops. Storms of red and orange climbed in the air, fell upon the trees beneath, setting their crowns blazing. A rush of heat tore through the clearing. Fire like this could reach down deep wells, overtake a galloping horse. What chance would they have in their feeble little trenches?

Danny was edging away, face twitching, moving towards the trees on the other side. The same terror flooded Garth, then he grabbed his friend's arm. "Stick together, okay? We're safest here. Stick together."

Danny started to jerk free, then stood still, mumbled something and nodded. The gray light was spreading fast. Eleven minutes since the helicopter set off. Come on!

The wind pressed again. More blazing needles swirled into the clearing, fell on the half-cleared ground near the edges, smoldered or went out. And back among the pine trunks, Garth saw the fire advancing.

Walls of flame glared through the smoke, rising and collapsing and rising again. Bursts of fire glared as resin-filled, super-heated pockets of air exploded. Red and orange threw themselves at trunks, ran up them like huge burning lizards, swarmed out along branches. Glowing needles flew on the wind; red-hot twigs and cones rained downwards. The speed of it! Garth managed to think. One moment, a tree stood whole against the blazing wall; next moment it was exploding and dying.

Radiant heat surged forty yards across the clearing at them. They ducked and covered their faces. "Pour water on a handkerchief!" Max bawled. "Or on your shirt. Breathe through that!"

Coughing, sputtering, Garth fumbled his water bottle from the pack. Fourteen minutes. The fire bellowed. "Here!" he gasped, and thrust the bottle at Isaac, who was dragging his T-shirt over his mouth.

Then more thundering sounded, straight above them, and the chopper swung in out of the half-dark.

It came in past the watch-tower, frighteningly close, curving around the high steel skeleton. It began to hover, the fire's light dancing on its olive-green body, bucking and jolting in the updrafts. Garth clamped his hands over his face as the rotors sent dirt and grit spraying around them. He couldn't see any crew.

Max stood halfway towards the far side of the clearing, arms high above his head in a signal, staggering in the wind. The helicopter side-slipped towards him, engine pounding, shuddering in the hot gusts that raced from the blazing trees. Smoke billowed by, and the machine half-vanished.

A door slid open in its side, and something spiraled down towards Max. The sling. Nobody was on it; they were probably all fighting to keep the chopper in the air.

"Ready—!" Max's yell came in fragments above the thunder of engines and flames. "Kels – irst!" The girl half-crouched beside her trench. Isaac gripped her arm; he looked ready to throw her right up into the helicopter.

From the trees, the fire surged forward. Two tall pines burst apart in a roar of burning air and exploding resin. Flames leaped almost horizontally across the clearing. A cloud of burning needles surrounded the chopper. It zoomed frantically upwards, empty sling dangling beneath it.

The whole front row of pines was blazing. Garth reeled against the pull of wind as the fire began sucking oxygen towards itself. Back eddies flung cones and branches in fiery arcs. All six of them were crouching and gaping, shocked faces lit red and orange.

The helicopter swung down again. More smoke poured past it. The two bellowing roars of engine and fire merged again. Isaac started urging, almost dragging Kelsey towards the sling. Her ankle twisted under her, and her mouth opened in a cry nobody could hear.

Another explosion of fire burst above the trees, soaring higher than the watch-tower. More radiant heat sent them cowering on the ground, Garth glimpsed a fireball racing towards the bucking helicopter, about to swallow it.

When he lifted his head a few seconds later, the chopper was climbing away, jolting and veering in the slamming wind-gusts, the sling smoking as it coiled upwards and in through the open door. The helicopter hung for a moment high above the clearing as if it was trying to say something; then it turned and flew away, fading into the murky dawn light. They were on their own.

FIFTEEN

Isaac still gripped Kelsey by her arm and waist while she slumped against him. Hinu knelt by her trench, hands to her face. Danny's whole body sagged.

Max stumbled towards them, shouting. Not at them – into his cellphone. Garth couldn't hear the words.

He couldn't hear anything above the great drum-beat of the fire. Around nearly the whole clearing now, trees flailed in the ferocious updrafts. More crowns exploded into sprays of flame, thick and orange-yellow in the middle, thinner red on the outside. Muddy, black-brown smoke tore through the sky. The wind flung itself in a different direction, and for half a second, Garth glimpsed shattered, toppling trunks and branches far back in the burning area. Then another front of radiant heat reached them, and he huddled on the ground like a trapped beast.

Max was yelling, louder than ever. "Get in the trenches! Pour your water on the dirt; drag it in on top of you. Face down. Hinu, Danny – get those parkas off!"

Instantly, people were moving: Isaac forcing Kelsey

back into her trench, grabbing his black helmet before sliding into his own; Hinu wriggling out of her parka, tossing it aside, diving into the ground. Only Danny hunched motionless, staring at the fire.

Garth grabbed his friend by the elbow again, shook him till his head wobbled. "Get the parka off. It'll melt and burn you! The fumes will poison you!" For a second, Danny didn't seem to recognize him; then his hands tore at the yellow fabric, pulling it from him.

Sparks landed on the sleeve of Garth's sweater. He brushed them off, whipped round to stare as the blazing top of a pine fell, rolling in flames towards the cabin and watch-tower. He dropped into his trench, kicking loose dirt into the corners, pulling more towards the rim. He felt the blisters on his hands and feet rip open once more, but it all seemed far away. His heart pounded, and a huge, desperate energy flooded him. There were stories of firefighters pulling whole trees aside to escape from fires; he could understand how.

The flames roared on, writhing storms of orange flaring and flailing among the trees, then standing still suddenly, rising in solid sheets as the ground itself seemed to catch fire. The cabin was burning now. Max was right; if they'd stayed there, they'd have been roasted alive. Another tree tore apart in flames, flinging gouts of burning needles and cones through the air. Branches whirled and clanged against the tower.

Garth crouched in his trench. "Hard hats!" Max bawled. "Put your hats on. Protect your head and neck!" Garth jammed his down harder. He seized his bottle and shook the last drops onto his filthy handkerchief, wadding it over nose and mouth. He knew not to breathe in super-heated air. It would sear the tissues inside his throat, and his chest muscles would lock shut, cutting off oxygen to his brain. That and radiant heat, plus the carbon monoxide in smoke, were what killed most people in forest fires. The flames reached them later, when they were already dead or unconscious.

The others had disappeared below ground, hugging the earth, faces buried in it. Only Max still crouched, yelling and jerking his arm at Garth to get down. Garth ducked, began huddling into the bottom of his trench, raking earth down on himself with his shovel. Then he lifted his head again. A force seemed to be dragging at him, pulling him up to watch the most terrible sight he'd ever seen.

Fires almost encircled the clearing now. The only gap was in the felled area, where dead branches smoldered. Garth remembered the deer – had it gotten away? Where to? He thought of Hinu's fleeing people. There were things he'd never known about or tried to understand. He knew that now.

Flames rushed up closer to him, as the roof of the cabin fell in. Sparks whirled across the clearing, and Garth ducked again. A crackling crash brought his head up once more. Another treetop lay blazing against the thin steel legs of the watch-tower. The struts were buckled where the falling timber had hit. The tower shook and shuddered from the impact.

At a corner of the tall pines, two fires met in a thundering column of flame. Garth held his breath as an orange pillar soared thirty yards into the air, booming and roaring. Fiery cones and branches that had been rolling towards him stopped and were sucked back into the firestorm. A gale of wind blew his hard hat from his head, hauled him almost out of the trench.

He forced himself down below ground, gloved hands clasped over his head. As he groveled face down, something hit the exposed back of his neck. Fire! he scrabbled at it, then realized it was cold. Dirt. No, a drop of rain. Another smacked against his half-turned cheek. Rain, at last and too late. Only days of it could stop the monster roaring around him.

Voices called from the other trenches, thin and feeble against the roll of flames. "Kelsey? You all right?" It was Hinu. The other girl replied, and Garth knew she was sobbing. Someone was calling his name now. Danny. "I'm okay!" Garth yelled back. "I'm—"

BLAM!! The explosion made Garth's whole body convulse. His head rammed into the hard clay at the end of his trench. For a second, he thought an entire row of tree crowns must have gone up together. Then he realized it was the cabin's gas stove. He heard the *clang*! as fragments hit the watch-tower, felt blazing shapes flash overhead.

He had to look, had to know what was happening. Carefully he lifted one hand above the rim of the trench. Radiant heat struck through his glove. He lowered his face, drew in a deep lungful of air through his filthy, water-damp T-shirt, and came to his knees, peering over the edge through eyes that were forced into slits.

The ring of fire was almost complete. In the smoking strip

of felled, now-blackened stumps and roots, steam rose as swirls of searing air baked the wet ground. Another raindrop fell uselessly on Garth's forehead as he watched.

The smashed remains of the wooden cabin lay in a burning mess against one corner of the watch-tower. One thin metal leg rose out of the flames, glowing dull red. It seemed to have bent – it couldn't be; must be the shimmer of heat. The sky above was a press of heavy black clouds, mixed with rolling, swelling smoke. Garth saw thin rain slanting down against the lines of fire. Too late, he thought again. Too little and too late.

More slams of wind. More whirls of fiery fragments through the air. Garth heard himself gag and cough as smoke billowed past. But his eyes were fixed on the glowing wreckage at the foot of the watch-tower.

Another blazing treetop sailed down, almost gracefully. It smashed into a big fallen branch, somersaulted just like the other branch that had come wheeling down the gully above the Pine, and hurtled into the red junk piled against the watch-tower. Fresh flames licked up the steel.

A new noise rose above the beat of the fires. A grinding, shrieking noise. Something in pain.

The tower lurched. It twisted and bent, a wounded animal searching for something to cling to. Garth saw the glowing leg peel apart like melted toffee. The steel frame toppled, slowly, then in a rushing plummet, straight towards their pathetic pits in the ground.

SIXTEEN

Garth flung himself into his trench, flattening himself down, trying somehow to scrabble under the earth. He felt dirt in his mouth, knew he was gaping in terror. His eyes were jammed shut, but they still held the image of the great steel shape toppling at him.

A colossal, clanging *BOOM!* right beside him, shook the whole clearing. Earth cascaded into the trench, half-covering him, filling his ears, pouring down the back of his sweater. A huge shape leapt across the ground above.

Screams rose from the trenches nearby. Danny was howling, "No! No!" Someone else yelled in agony, then the voice cut off.

Garth began clawing his way out of the collapsing trench, shoving earth aside. He saw Isaac struggling from his own trench, and Hinu also scrabbling her way out into the open, dirt showering from her. He jerked round as a branch or something bounced suddenly onto the ground nearby, smoking and rolling. He heard himself yell as he saw it was Danny, tumbling over and over, fragments of glowing steel dropping from his clothes as he beat and thumped at himself.

Garth snatched the shovel that lay beside his trench, hurdled a yard-long piece of smoking steel, and landed beside his friend, flinging dirt over Danny's clothes where they smoldered, whacking with the shovel blade at the back of his sweater where smoke rose.

It was a few seconds before he understood that Danny's thrashing arms and yells of "No! No!" were now aimed at him. Then Isaac barged into him, wrestling the shovel away. "You trying to kill him?"

The boy's eyes glared. There was a gouge in the side of his stupid black helmet. Garth saw his own hard hat on the ground nearby, and grabbed it as Danny pushed himself up. The three of them flinched as heat and smoke drove past. Danny stood shakily, smacking at his ripped, scorched clothes.

The clearing was a shambles. The top two-thirds of the watch-tower lay in buckled pieces across it, sticking out of the ground like ugly spears. Stumps of tower legs rose from the crackling, flaring wreckage of cabin and trees. The very top of the tower had smashed into pines on the far side of the clearing, and burning branches lay strewn across the ground. Around their ruined refuge, the fires boomed on. More heat rushed past.

Isaac began trying to kick pieces of hot metal away from the trenches. It's no good, thought Garth; they're half caved in, anyway. Hinu and Kelsey huddled together on the ground close by. In the hellish orange glow, Garth saw they were crying. No, it was the rain on their faces. The useless rain.

They hunched as wind sent more branches tumbling and flaring past. The fire had them now. Heat or smoke or the bombardment of blazing, broken trees: it was going to get them. Where—?

Someone pulled at Garth's arm. Another tree exploded. Sparks flowered up, scudded down onto the clearing and their bent backs. Smoke streamed over them, doubling them up with coughing.

The hand kept pulling at Garth's arm. Isaac – pointing at a log-sized chunk of metal on the ground. Horror gripped Garth as he realized it lay across Max's trench.

The three boys blundered across to the smoking steel. They heaved at it, mouths wide open, eyes unfocused, gloved hands wrenching. Hopeless. They couldn't shift something this big.

More hands seized it. Hinu and Kelsey, the blonde girl half-crawling. Impossibly, the steel moved, gouging a furrow across the clay as it slid. Max lay motionless in his trench, almost buried. Only a hand and part of one leg showed. The hand twitched, then was still.

Isaac flung himself at the piled dirt, scooping it out with his hands. Garth joined him. Another of Max's hands appeared. The back of his head. Trees exploded on two sides of the clearing, and their ears rang with the noise. Cinders and hot needles rained past. Garth yelped and smacked at his cheek.

There was blood in Max's hair, clotted with dirt, thick and dark and welling. His hard hat lay half-buried beside him, gashed and buckled. "Max!" It was his own voice shouting, Garth realized. "Max!" Both hands twitched this time, then went limp once more.

They hauled the big man half-upright in the trench, gasping at his weight. Hinu and Danny grabbed his arms, dragged him over the edge and onto the ash-covered ground. Kelsey pushed away smoldering twigs as Max flopped like a bundle of rags. Blood pulsed and flowed from the back of his head. Then his legs moved feebly, and Garth sobbed with relief.

The relief didn't last. Another surge of heat sent them face-down on the ground, covering their ears and heads. Trees were disintegrating, collapsing into the clearing from all sides. Flames poured upwards in dizzying waves, dredging air into them. Walls of fire bellowed around the clearing. They couldn't last against this. They were going to die.

A hand pulled at him again. He swung round, and saw Hinu. She was shouting words he couldn't understand, thrusting with her arm towards the edge of the clearing. The wind veered yet again, smoke flicked away, and Garth saw she was pointing at the felled strip between the rows of pines.

No use. Smoke and radiant heat would get them there, too. Red-hot twigs and needles were scudding across.

Then Garth remembered the deer. In his mind, he saw it again, turning to look at them, bounding away down the felled area. A huge force swelled somewhere inside him. Next second, he was yelling at the others.

"The felled part! Head for the felled part! We can get behind the firefront. We'll dig ourselves in there!"

Isaac understood instantly. He grabbed one of Max's arms as the supervisor stirred again. Danny and Kelsey gaped from scorched, smeared faces. Then Danny nodded. "I'll help – Kelsey!"

"She—" Garth began, but Danny stopped him. "I'll kick her butt all the way if I have to." His face was calm, and Garth understood that his friend had pushed his terror away again, somewhere inside. Another surge of affection filled him. He could almost have hugged Danny – but guys didn't do that kind of thing, either.

He stared at the ground ahead. Forty...fifty yards to cross. Heat and smoke all the way. A litter of burning cones and branches for the last part, with the wind flinging more to join them all the time. The final twenty yards were going to be like fire-walking. They had to keep going, no matter what.

Kelsey brandished her water bottle at him. "Some – left. Pour it on handkerchiefs – breathe through."

"No!" Garth shook his head. "Not so near the fire. You'd be sucking in steam. Cover your face, but no water!"

He snatched another look at the shimmering oven ahead. "Grab hold of one another. Just go. Don't stop. Go!"

They crouched in two groups by the side of their smashed trenches. Danny and Hinu with their arms around Kelsey. Garth and Isaac, each gripping Max by a shoulder and sleeve. Garth dragged in a lungful of air for what lay ahead.

One of Max's gloves had fallen off. Garth couldn't see it anywhere. The man's legs and head moved now as he tried to stand. He was mumbling; Garth and Isaac bent to listen, and heard half-words. "Go . . . you go."

"Shut your face!" Isaac yelled, right into the supervisor's ear. "Just move!"

Trees roared and broke open behind them. Heat struck at their backs. Wind blew the smoke away once more, and there was the thin zone of felled land.

"Now!" Garth shouted. "Now!"

They scuttled forward like crabs. Hinu, Danny and Kelsey first, bent in half, staggering over the uneven clay, Kelsey shrieking and swearing as her left leg pushed at the ground. Behind them, Garth and Isaac, hauling at Max, struggling to stay upright. The man's feet moved feebly; after just ten steps, his weight had them gasping and groaning.

The flames swelled to meet them. The awful drum-roll pounded in their ears. Garth stumbled on a smoking branch, fought to keep upright as Max's body slumped towards the ground, reeled on. Heat burned his lungs. Rain or sparks – he couldn't tell which – stung his cheeks. Burning twigs pattered on his hard hat.

He felt the skin on his face tighten and begin to blister. He was shouting wildly as he staggered on, calling to his mother and father, praying and yelling. The three ahead had disappeared into a bank of sooty smoke. Even if they made it to the felled area, they couldn't be sure of safety, Garth knew.

Max was pushing harder with his legs now, trying to help. Garth's heart pounded. Strength was draining out of him; he couldn't keep going. He howled as burning ash hit his neck and clung there. Heat struck up from the ground at his blistered feet.

More wind. The smoke in front shredded, and he saw

the other three. They'd reached the felled strip. Hinu and Kelsey were slumped in a bare patch between two stumps. Danny was hauling himself upright, turning towards Garth.

Then a storm of burning pine needles whirled across the clearing, covering Danny and the girls. Hinu screamed, began flailing with both hands at her face.

Garth's head went down as heat blasted at them, too. From the corner of his eye, he saw Isaac's foot tread on a burning pine-cone. The boy's leg twisted, and he fell. Max crashed face-down onto the smoldering earth.

The back of the man's jacket was smoking. The skin of his gloveless hand had begun peeling in red strips. Garth and Isaac dropped to their knees beside him, clutching at his arms. A billow of black smoke set them coughing uncontrollably. Garth's eyes streamed; he could barely see. He tried to drag Max up again, felt Isaac doing the same. But they couldn't move him.

A roar and a crash near them. Flames poured by. A red mist seemed to fill Garth's head. He crouched, helpless. Done.

Different hands hauled at him and Max. Danny was there, snarling and shouting, teeth bared. "Come on! Come *on!*"

Somehow Garth could stand. Somehow he could pull. With Max draped across their shoulders, the three boys reeled the last yards into the felled area. As they staggered through the remains of a glowing branch, Garth felt the sides of his boots begin to melt and drop away. Fresh pain clawed at his feet, became part of the agony that racked his body. Then they were through, and collapsed beside

Kelsey and Hinu.

They huddled on the ground, choking and crying. It's not enough, Garth knew. The felled area was smaller than he'd thought. Smoke and heat still rushed at them. He forced himself onto hands and knees, and felt the fury of the flames claw at him. A dead branch nearby smoked and glowed. He tried to crawl away from it, but his body wouldn't answer.

Hinu's face was raw and speckled with black where the needles had clung and burned. Isaac half-knelt, half-sprawled, staring at her. "Oh, no!" Garth heard him sobbing. "Oh, no!"

It was going to end here. The smoke would get them first, or one of the airless vacuums as the fire sucked all oxygen into it. Maybe one of them might – he tried to lift his head, look around at the others. The fire thundered once more. Rain drops struck at him as his eyes met Danny's.

Then the rain was smashing on him, slamming down on him like waves, flattening him to the ground. He was drenched in a second. The glowing branch turned to a sodden blackness.

Danny's face was near his, dripping hair plastered across it, trying to speak. Garth opened his own mouth, heard another booming and roaring. A second deluge of water crashed onto him, filling his mouth, knocking him into the dirt that was now streaming mud.

A glorious coolness covered him. This couldn't be – what was…? He glimpsed Isaac yelling, pointing at the sky. Hinu stared up, eyes enormous in her scorched face.

He managed to turn his own neck. Just ten yards above him, a second chopper banked away, climbing after the first. A third was already curving in, huge bucket swaying beneath it, water slopping and pouring over the bucket's edge. Underneath it they crouched, exhausted, hurt, alive.

SEVENTEEN

He had first degree burns on his face and neck, the doctor told Garth. They hurt, and they looked red and swollen. A few second-degree burns on his feet where his boots had started to melt; these burns had damaged tissue deeper down that the blisters had already exposed. They didn't hurt so much, funnily enough. The doctor said that was because nerve endings had been partly destroyed. They'd heal, but he'd have to limp carefully for a while.

And Hinu would have to smile carefully for a bit. The burns to her face were superficial only; peeling patches dotted her cheeks and forehead, but they would soon fade. Garth felt glad, and knew why.

The others were much the same, except for Max. He had twenty stitches in the back of his head. ("His hard head," said Kelsey). His hard hat had saved him. There were third-degree burns on one hand, searing right down through layers to the tissue beneath. The doctors were taking skin grafts from other places ("He won't tell me where!" Kelsey complained), but he would have scars forever.

Maybe they all would. Scars of a different sort. Through

the first nights in hospital, Garth heard Danny moaning with nightmares. Garth jerked and kicked out of his own dreams where flames came at him from all sides. He could tell from Isaac's breathing that the other boy was lying awake in the darkness.

A procession of people came to see them. Leah and the kids from her gang stared at the bandages and dressings that covered cheeks and hands. "Doesn't it hurt?" some of the girls asked. Garth started to say, "Not really," but then said, "I can handle it," and saw Leah grinning to herself.

In spite of her ankle, Kelsey was first out of bed. She came hobbling into the room where the three boys lay. "Knock!" Danny told her. "We might not be decent!" Kelsey grinned. "That's why I didn't knock."

"Hey," she went on. "The Hawaii trip's still on." And, as Danny and Garth gaped at her, and Isaac looked at the bedclothes, "We've been in the papers and on TV. People are calling in with donations. The airline's gonna give us special rates."

She grinned again. "Be good to go someplace tropical, don't you think?"

Garth's parents came twice a day, sometimes more. His mother wept the first time she saw his burned face and bandaged feet. His father squeezed his shoulder (Garth managed not to yell; every bit of his body ached), and went, "Son...son..." By the time he'd told them twenty times that he was okay his mother looked as if she might believe it some day.

"I've been to Bald Dome," his father said on the fourth morning, just after the doctors had told Garth he'd be going home in a couple of days. "How you ever managed to get out of there..." Garth's dad shook his head.

"Hinu did it." The words were out before Garth had time to think them. "She – her people knew. I dunno how." In another world raging with fire and heat, he saw the deer turn, then bound off into the felled area.

His mother watched him for a second, then nodded. His father stared, and glanced sideways at Garth's mom. "They... well, sounds like something to talk about, son."

They left, his mother giving him a smile from the door. At that moment, Kelsey limped in on crutches, ready to go home.

"How's the ankle?" Danny asked her.

The girl grinned. Her blonde hair had been cut so the burned parts hardly showed at all. "No worries. I'll be able to beat the guys again in about a week."

She stared across at Isaac, who was watching her, and got quiet. This time it was Garth and Danny's turn to look at the bedclothes. "You want to let your hair grow longer," she told him finally. "It would look good on you."

They were on television, all right. Garth and Danny finally saw it on the mid-day news in the ward's TV room, Danny chewing on his fourth granola bar of the morning. "Two youths are to be charged with trespassing and breaching Fire Safety Regulations," the woman announcer said. Garth felt glad Isaac wasn't with them. The other boy never left their room, except to go to the bathroom.

They stared as the camera panned over zone after zone of blackened dead pines. The rain had come just in time to help fire crews stop the blaze from crossing another river and rampaging through valleys of new pines. After nearly twenty-four hours of rain, the burned areas still smoked. Ridges and plateaus flowed past on the screen – a filthy wasteland of ash, charred trunks and smoldering branches, which seemed as if it would never end.

It would be years and years till the forest was healed again. Years and years, and millions of dollars. The stories Garth had imagined himself telling to impress kids at school didn't seem important any longer. All of Kinross was suffering, including his dad, Garth knew. "There are trees that live for five thousand years," he'd said when he came to see Garth the second or third time. "Then people do something like this, and…I don't know." Garth nodded; Isaac would have to live with this all his life.

Be a while till some of us heal too, Garth knew. How would Danny feel about going into a forest again? How would any of them feel? When would there *be* a forest for them to go into?

He leaned forward as the camera paused at the edge of a ruined zone. In the churned-up ground at its edge, where bulldozers and fire-trucks had battled to hold the flames back, a single, self-sown little pine stood, alive and unharmed.

Then he and Danny exclaimed together. The view had changed to a ridge of young trees that the blaze had hardly reached. Near a patch of open ground, something moved. Spooked by the helicopter, a deer wheeled round and disappeared back into the pines.

Danny and Hinu were discharged next. They hadn't needed much treatment – "just a head transplant," Danny told people.

Hinu didn't come into the room where the three boys were. Garth tried to imagine how she was feeling about Isaac; how Isaac felt about her. Mostly, he just hoped that Isaac would get that ATV-building place, sometime and somewhere.

It wasn't till Danny had gone to see if the hospital still had his fire-burned, shovel-battered sweater (he wanted to wear it to school, he said), that Garth had the chance to ask Hinu about something else.

"That deer," he said, as they sat in the TV room.

Hinu's brown eyes watched him. "What about it?"

"How did you know to follow...? Did your grandfather...?" Garth stopped and felt silly.

Hinu snorted. "Deer aren't *that* smart! I just thought that if an animal could find a way out, we intelligent life-forms could, too. Me and Kelsey, I mean."

She smiled at him, tucking her hair back behind neat ears. Garth remembered again those moments in the little gully and on the hillside. Maybe he'd never know.

The girl was still looking at him, her face serious now. The burn marks on her smooth cheeks were fading. "Tell Isaac good luck, huh?" Garth nodded.

Later, he watched her and Danny walk out of the ward together. Sometime, when things were back to normal, he'd have to start thinking out ways of getting Hinu to walk places with *him*. That might give his dad something else to talk about.

"Those choppers that found you are still dumping water

113

on hot spots," Garth's dad told him that evening, when he dropped clothes off for Garth to wear home the next day. "They must have just about drained the Pine dry."

Gangs were working through the burned zones, moving in from the edges, digging over smoldering parts and spraying them with water from backpack pumps, turning charred logs so they wouldn't roll downhill and maybe start new fires. Every smoking patch had to be cleared out properly. Fires could flare up again after smoldering for six months or more.

Garth pictured the trees where they'd been pruning, just...five? six days before. The slim gray trunks and bright green needles; the scent of resin and clean cold air; chickadees darting among shafts of sunlight. The fire had smashed through there as well. How long till it was a place of life again?

Hardly anyone had been to see Isaac. His father hadn't come. A woman Garth knew must be his mother was there twice, crying as she hurried from the room. The police arrived one day; two of them talked to Isaac in low voices. Garth headed off to the TV room.

On the sixth or seventh afternoon, another guy their age came into the room. He didn't look at Garth; went and stood awkwardly by Isaac's bed. Garth had seen him for a few moments only, by the crashed ATV, but he recognized the dark hair instantly. The guy stayed maybe five minutes; neither he nor Isaac seemed to have much to say. As he went out, he shot a glance at Garth and mumbled, "Sorry." Garth just nodded.

Isaac did have one other visitor. Not long after Garth's father had dropped off his clothes, Max limped into the room. A football-sized mass of bandages covered his head; a soccer-ball-sized mass covered one hand. "Who's gonna finish the pruning if you lazy guys stay in bed?" he demanded.

He talked for a bit to Garth, then he limped over and sat by Isaac's bed. "A lot of people are gonna tell you how you messed up, son," Garth heard as he pretended to read. "But you did some amazing things, and I'm not gonna forget that. I've been talking to the cops" – Garth felt Isaac jerk at the word – "If they give you community service or whatever, maybe you can work it out doing replanting and stuff. In the meantime, you face up to what you did wrong, eh? Then you keep going the way you showed you can."

A sound made Garth glance sideways. Isaac was crying. After a moment, Garth headed off to the TV room again.

When Garth had finished getting dressed to go home next morning, it was Isaac who sat in bed pretending to read. His mother had asked if he could stay in the hospital for a while, Garth's own mom had told him that Isaac's father didn't want him at home – not yet, anyway. The court case was coming up sometime. Until then, Garth had no idea what would happen.

His parents were waiting in the corridor. Garth had just told his mother another couple of times that he was okay. Isaac's eyes stayed on the car magazine in his lap.

"I'll see you," Garth said.

Isaac didn't look up. "Yeah."

Garth was silent for a second. "I mean it. Might be a

while, but I'll see you. Right?"

Now the other boy's head lifted. His face changed. His mouth became firmer. "Right. Thanks. Thanks, Garth."

It was the first time Isaac had spoken his name.

"Making a bit of a detour on the way home," Garth's father announced as they drove away from the hospital.

Garth gazed out of the window at the glittering day. "Where?"

"The Katenes'," his mother said. "Hinu's house."

Garth's head jerked around. Heck, she was smiling at him in the mirror! He gazed out of the window again, trying to look as if he wasn't interested. "What's happening?"

"Her grandpa organized it," his mother told him. Garth heard his father clear his throat in an embarrassed sort of way. His mother was still smiling.

"It's a tradition with their people," his mom went on. "There's lots of wounds to heal, but new life is starting again. The most important thing is that you were all saved. So the Katenes would like you and Danny and Kelsey to be there. Isaac..." she paused. "Some things need more time."

Garth kept looking out of the window. He hoped the bandages on his cheek would make him look like a real wounded soldier. "So what are the Katenes going to be doing?"

"Oh," his mother said, "didn't I tell you? They're planting a tree."